**Large Print Roz
Roszel, Renee.
Surrender to a playboy**

SURRENDER TO
A PLAYBOY

SURRENDER TO A PLAYBOY

BY

RENEE ROSZEL

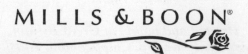

For Shirley Casey, Doug Shipe and
Barbara Bancroft Richardson, fab folks who came
when I yelled, "Help!"

*First published in Great Britain 2003
Large Print edition 2003
Harlequin Mills & Boon Limited,
Eton House, 18-24 Paradise Road,
Richmond, Surrey TW9 1SR*

© Renee Roszel Wilson 2003

ISBN 0 263 17944 3

*Set in Times Roman 15½ on 16½ pt.
16-1003-62783*

*Printed and bound in Great Britain
by Antony Rowe Ltd, Chippenham, Wiltshire*

CHAPTER ONE

THE moment Taggart Lancaster stepped out of his rental car he would become an impostor—a black sheep and prodigal son—returning home after an absence of sixteen years.

Taggart stared out through the windshield at the elegant Victorian home with its wooden gingerbread and angled bay windows, a russet jewel in a setting of evergreen. Clutching the steering wheel, his knuckles white with tension, he cursed himself. What was he doing? What had possessed him to agree to such a wild stunt?

His gaze drifted over the turreted and steeply gabled roof. Moody and silent, he took in the high-country beauty of the American Rocky Mountains, an unspoiled wilderness of piney forests, striated cliffs, steep divides and rainbowed waterfalls. Distant, snowcapped peaks loomed in all directions, soaring into a boundless summer sky.

Bonner Wittering, Taggart's oldest friend and most time-consuming legal client, had said Colorado's Rockies were beautiful. Taggart was reminded of the Swiss Alps, and the remote

5

boarding school, where they both grew up. A wave of nostalgia washed over him and he fought it off. That "we-two-against-the-world" baggage is what got him into this mess.

He did need a vacation, though. That had been another of Bonner's arguments. The way things stood, Bonner couldn't come, couldn't leave Boston as a condition of his bail. Due to the fact that Bonn owned a condo in Paris, the court felt he represented a flight risk.

As Bonner's lawyer, Taggart knew how un-amused bail bondsmen were when one of their clients jumped bail. As an officer of the court, Taggart couldn't allow Bonner to leave town. Which Bonn swore was exactly what he'd do if given no other choice.

Taggart shook his head, muttering, "I must be nuts." Nobody else on earth could have talked him into such a bizarre plan. But Taggart and Bonn were closer than most real brothers. Unfortunately for Taggart's argument against the plan, they actually did look enough alike to be mistaken for siblings.

"Bonn, old buddy, I can't decide who's the bigger fool," he groused. "You, for being such a gullible boob, or me, for agreeing to this—this *idiocy*."

He spent another interminable moment strangling the leather-swathed steering wheel. "It's no crime to do a favor for a friend," he muttered. "You're just here to make a sick old lady happy." He flexed his fingers to relieve cramped muscles. "So *move!* Get out of the *blasted* car!" Shoving his misgivings aside, he sucked in a deep breath and flung open the door.

Gravel crunched beneath his polished wing tips as he stepped out onto the drive.

The charade had begun.

He grabbed his suitcase from the car trunk, strode across the drive and up the wooden steps to the wraparound porch. His footfalls echoed on redwood, sounding like threatening thunder. For the thousandth time he shook off nagging misgivings for agreeing to Bonner's plea. Banging out some of his frustration on the heavy lion's head knocker, he announced his arrival with the finesse of a machine gun.

"She won't be able to tell you're not Bonn," he mumbled. "He was nineteen the last time he was here. People change. Besides, she's practically blind and deaf." Even if she weren't, he and Bonn both had black hair, brown eyes and were approximately the same height, though at six-three Taggart was an inch taller. They were equally athletic and hit the gym several times a week for their regular racquetball game and weight training. They both played basketball in an amateur league. Besides their physical likeness, Taggart knew Bonner's history as well as he knew his own. He could do this favor for his friend—cheer an ailing grandmother whose fondest wish was to see her only living relative—just once more.

He winced. Well, she would believe he was her relative. That would make her happy, and *that's* what counted.

The front door opened to reveal a well-rounded, solid woman in a floral print dress. She looked to be in her mid-forties with a sprinkling of gray in her short, curly mop of brown hair. The expression she wore on her square face and small, plain features, was polite, but cool. ''Mr. Wittering?'' she queried in a tone that didn't sound like she'd been looking forward to meeting him.

Taggart nodded. ''I'm a little late. My flight...'' He let it drop. Delayed flights were more the norm than the exception.

''Yes, we checked.''

Taggart sensed there had been a moment of alarm in the Wittering household. Had they suspected Bonn had once again decided to disappoint his grandmother in favor of some new, impromptu escapade? The thought made him annoyed with himself for not easing their minds with a phone call. But the delay had only been an hour, and he'd made up time on the road. He supposed the truth was, he'd had his mind on his own dementia, agreeing to play out this little drama. "I'm sorry," he said. "I should have phoned."

"That would have been nice," she said, snappishly. Taggart didn't blame her for her attitude. On the contrary, he took pity on the woman, possibly the caregiver who'd doggedly written to Bonn, begging him to visit his grandmother. She clearly cared for her employer and was fiercely protective of her feelings.

"I'd like to see my grandmother as soon as possible," he said, assuming a repentant grandson would.

The woman's expression eased slightly, the taut slash that was her mouth softening but not quite curving into a smile. "After I show you to your room, I'll let Miz Witty know you're anxious to see her."

Ah, yes, *Miz Witty*. That's what Bonn always called her.

The woman waved him forward and stepped out of his way. "I'm Mrs. Kent, the housekeeper. Everybody calls me Ruby."

"It's nice to meet you, Ruby." He followed her through the foyer to the stairs. He didn't have much time to look around, but his impression was of furnishings that were a blend of modern with antiques; ceramic pottery and art abounded. He guessed they were original pieces collected over the years.

The place had a homey, welcoming feel, smelling of furniture polish and what he could only describe as—women—the scent left lingering in the air from flower arranging, scented baths and candles. His home had once smelled very much like this, until Annalisa—

"This is your room, Mr. Wittering," Ruby said, interrupting his melancholy reverie. She halted at the top of the stairs and opened a door.

"Call me—Bonn." He looked away, made a pained face at the sour taste that lie left in his mouth. *Get used to it, Tag,* he counseled himself. *You're going to be Bonner Wittering for the next two weeks.*

"If you insist—Bonn," she said as he shifted to face her again. "Miz Witty's room is across the hall toward the back of the house. I'll let her know you've arrived. Take a few minutes to freshen up, then go see her."

"Thank you, Ruby." He moved past her into a sunny room, obviously intended to make a guest both comfortable and at ease. The furnishings were influenced by the Shaker tradition of simplicity, left natural with a hand-rubbed oil finish. Bright rag rugs dotted the pine planks. In front of the lace-swathed window, a colorful bouquet of fresh flowers and greenery sat on a drop-leaf table, filling the room with sweetness.

He set down his bag and turned to the house-keeper to compliment the accommodations, but she no longer stood in the doorway. He peered out into the hall to glimpse her as she disappeared into to Miz Witty's room, no doubt to make the big announcement—*the prodigal has returned!*

Or so they thought.

Taggart decided to give Miz Witty a few minutes to prepare for his arrival, so he unpacked his suitcase and put away his things. He opted not to change out of his business suit, though he didn't recall Bonn ever wearing one, except when he'd been best man at Taggart's wedding to Annalisa, and, then, three years later—at her funeral. But Miz Witty wouldn't know how Bonn dressed. The last time she'd seen him, he'd surely been wearing a suit. After all it had been Bonn's parents' funeral, after their tragic deaths in an avalanche while they'd been cross-country skiing.

He ran a hand through his hair, not so much to move it out of his eyes, but to give his aggravation and frustration an outlet. Putting a fist through the wall didn't seem like the best plan.

Catching his scowl in the dresser mirror, he adjusted his expression and left the room. It was time. He'd put it off long enough. He walked to Miz Witty's door and knocked. The ''Come in,'' he heard had a melodious ring to it, as though the person speaking were exhilarated. He swatted down a fresh surge of self-loathing and turned the knob, pushing open the door.

His attention went immediately to the center-piece of the room, a large bed with a tall, ornately carved headboard and shorter but equally ornate footboard. The bedspread was a fusion of white silk, lace and brocade, giving the impression of a wintertime landscape. In the midst of all that snowy finery, reclining against a multitude of pillows, lounged a petite, queenlike woman with ivory skin and a smile so reminiscent of Bonn's it gave Taggart pause. Her eyes were large and iron-brown, her bone structure classic. Powder-white hair crowned her head in a groomed mound of wispy curls. Taggart thought she was an attractive, youthful-looking woman, even days away from her seventy-fifth birthday. Her white, silk dressing gown frothed with lace at the neck and wrists.

She held out her arms, looking like a human-size China doll, come to life. "My Bonny!" Those brown eyes grew liquid with what Taggart knew were tears of joy. He was struck with an urge to be transported telepathically back to Boston for an instant, just to kick Bonn in his backside for neglecting this fragile-looking doll of a woman. Without further hesitation, he moved across the Persian rug and leaned over the bed, allowing her to take him in her embrace. He held her gently, inhaling her scent, talcum powder and French milled soap.

"It's good to see you, Miz Witty," he murmured against her cool cheek. "You're looking marvelous." He'd seen her picture among the few Bonn kept. She was older by at least a decade than the photograph he remembered, and from what Bonn had said about her failing health, Taggart was surprised she looked so well. As for being blind and deaf, well, she certainly wasn't blind. She didn't even seem to need glasses. He wasn't sure about her hearing, yet. But she'd apparently heard his knock, which hadn't been particularly loud. "How are you?" he asked in his normal voice, a test to see if she could hear him.

"Just wonderful. My right leg is still too weak for me to stand, since my last stroke, and the pneumonia wasn't a cakewalk, but I'm getting stronger every day." She grasped his upper arms and held him just far enough away to look at him up close. Smiling, she scanned his face. With great difficulty Taggart held on to his pleasant expression. Did she see well enough to realize he wasn't Bonn? He experienced a creeping unease spiced with another bout of irritation. A part of him almost hoped she wasn't fooled. He hated the lie.

She touched his cheek, her small, cool hand fondly caressing. "You're even more handsome than I remember."

He shifted uneasily, not sure how to answer.

A slight cough or throat-clearing from somewhere behind him caught his attention. He turned. A striking woman stood not far away, her attention focused on Miz Witty. She wore blue jeans, a pink T-shirt and sneakers. In her hands she carried a tray containing a china teapot, matching cup and saucer and a plate of toast. He straightened, surprised at her almost magical appearance. He hadn't heard her come in.

"Oh, Bonny, darling," Miz Witty said, "this is my live-in health care provider, Mary O'Mara. Mary, this is my grandson, Bonner."

The woman with the tray shifted her attention to him, nodded and smiled politely. "How do you do, Mr. Wittering." Her voice was soft and on the sexy side of husky. She moved forward, hardly making a sound. She almost seemed to float. Taggart found himself staring, watching the graceful economy of her movements.

Her hair was long and loose, straight and black, parted in the middle. The shiny, undulating curtain swayed with every step she took, brushing each side of her face in turn—left, right, left, right. Watching her hair sway, nuzzling those rosy cheeks in alternating beats, was strangely hypnotic.

When she reached him she looked directly into his face, her eyes a striking shade of gray-brown—like smoke. They seemed to flash, as though a lightning storm raged beneath the dusky veil. "Please, excuse me, Mr. Wittering," she said, her husky tone as gracious as her smile.

He belatedly realized he was in her way, and stepped aside, feeling like a simpleton. "Pardon me."

"Absolutely no problem," she murmured, turning her pretty face away to attend to Miz Witty. "We're out of orange marmalade," she said, removing the silver lid from a dainty, cut-crystal container. "I hope strawberry jam is all right."

"Perfect! Delightful!" Miz Witty's light laugh tinkled like a bell. Taggart felt her cool fingers entwine with his. "Nothing could bother me to-day." She squeezed his fingers affectionately. "I'm so happy, I could burst. My Bonny has come home, at last."

Taggart tore his gaze from the young woman to look at Miz Witty. Tears welled in her eyes. His gut twisting with guilt, he gently squeezed her fingers in return, but was unable to conjure a smile.

"I'm so glad you're happy," Mary O'Mara said, her attention shifting to Taggart. She smiled. The beauty of it touched something inside him that he hadn't believed could be touched, ever again. Not after his Annalisa died.

He wasn't a man who smiled much, but he found himself on the brink as he took in this raven-haired woman with the smoky eyes. "I hope you enjoy your visit, Mr. Wittering," she said. Her throaty voice was only a whisper, yet it rang loud and long in his head.

"Call me Bonn," he said, feeling like a tongue-tied schoolboy.

"Thank you." She broke eye contact to face Miz Witty. "Can I get you anything else?"

"No, dear. Go relax for a while." The older woman poured tea into her cup, then paused. Her brows dipped in a thoughtful frown. "Oh—where are my manners?" She shifted to face Taggart. "Bonny, sweetheart, would you like some tea? Perhaps a snack after your long trip?" Without letting him respond she waved a negating hand. "Of course, you would." She faced Mary. "Dear, please ask Cook for another plate of toast and more tea."

"Right away," Mary said with a smile as she turned to go.

"If you've got coffee…" Taggart broke in, experiencing a prick of disappointment that she was leaving. "I'll serve myself and bring it back here. I'm not hungry."

Mary looked at Taggart. "Don't trouble yourself, sir. I'll get it."

"Absolutely not." He turned to Miz Witty. "I'll be right back." He was having trouble with the idea of seeing Mary O'Mara walk away.

Miz Witty smiled and took up her teacup. "That's very gentlemanly of you, Bonny." Sipping she beamed at Mary, then added, "He's truly a treasure."

The young woman smiled at her employer, nodded and shifted to leave, her sneakers soundless as she glided away. Taggart followed her out the door, closing it as he left. Her scent drifted back to him, light and floral, seeming to beckon.

Suddenly, Taggart found it essential to see those eyes again, experience the invigorating warmth of her smile. He had not been gripped by such an unexpected need since that night he'd met Annalisa, and he'd never expected to experience anything even vaguely as intoxicating, ever again. He and Annalisa had fallen in love the night they'd met. They were married three weeks later, so the courtship lasted about as long as it took for them to eat dinner. By dessert they'd been engaged.

For a long time after his wife's death he hadn't dated at all. After three years, his friends finally

convinced him to get out, meet women. Since
then he hadn't been a monk, but he wasn't a playboy like Bonn.

His work kept him busy. If the truth were
known, he was more accustomed to being pursued
than pursuing. That's why, when he saw Mary
O'Mara, the sense of urgency that overtook him
was startling, even strangely disturbing. Where
had the dour, guarded Taggart Lancaster suddenly
gone? He'd never been the sort to chase females
down. Certainly, he'd never experienced such a
strong craving to speak to a woman since
Annalisa's death. He'd never even imagined he
would.

"Mary?" He caught up with her, "May I call
you Mary?" he asked with a smile. "So you're
the Mary who wrote those letters to—me."

At the head of the stairs she halted abruptly and
shifted to face him. Those beautiful eyes he'd so
badly wanted to gaze into again staggered him
with their shocking transformation. Her stare was
withering, her eyes flaring with fury and malice.

"Yes, I am *that* Mary." That sexy voice he'd
wanted to hear again had become low and hard-
edged. "How dare you neglect that wonderful
woman for so many years, you—*you selfish
snake!*"

Taggart stood there, speechless. Her metamorphosis from sweet to spiteful had been so swift and fierce, he was caught completely off guard.

"For Miz Witty's sake," she went on in a deadly whisper, "When you and I are in the same room with her, I will be polite and *pretend* to find you less than thoroughly repulsive. I will call you Bonn in her presence, if that is her wish, and I will try not to spit in your eye when you call me Mary. But otherwise, Mr. Wittering," she hissed, *"stay out of my way!"*

CHAPTER TWO

TAGGART watched Mary O'Mara-of-the-smoky-eyes storm down the stairs. The air around him still sizzled with her rage, and he thought he could detect the faint aroma of charred ego. Now he knew how a tree felt when struck by lightning and left a smoldering stump.

Absently loosening his tie, he muttered, "That went well." Being a lawyer, he was accustomed to adversarial relationships, but he hadn't seen that one coming. *And why not, idiot?* Hadn't she written letters for the past two years, pleading for Bonn to come, getting rejection after rejection? What kind of attitude did he think she'd have? Taggart was usually good at gauging people, sensing their sincerity or lack of it. Plainly, something in her smile or those smoky eyes had jammed his radar. That tongue-lashing he'd just been given had hit him like a two-by-four to the back of his skull.

"So far I've been greeted with suspicion, devotion and loathing." He stuffed his hands into his slacks pockets, muttering, "Thanks a whole heap, Bonn, old buddy."

20

He took the stairs two at a time. He had no desire to get coffee, but he'd told Miz Witty that's what he was going to do, so he might as well. Maybe a strong cup of java would wash the taste of Miss O'Mara's bone-jarring disgust out of his mouth.

At the bottom of the staircase, he swung toward the back of the house, assuming that's where he'd find the kitchen. He was right. Upon entering, though, he was surprised to see Miss I-Hate-Your-Guts O'Mara along with another woman who stood on the opposite side of the kitchen, a heavy-boned blonde who appeared to be about his age. She was pretty, but not nearly as stunning as Mary.

When the blonde spotted him, she arched her penciled brows in triangles and gave him a thorough once-over. Miss O'Mara did exactly the opposite. She turned her back, her rigid spine and shoulders telegraphing her antagonism. He tried to shake off his aggravation at her transparent resentment at his intrusion. She knew he was getting coffee. Where did she think he would go for it, Brazil?

''Well, hello there.'' The blonde turned away from the stove to fully face him. With a wooden stirring spoon in her hand, she crossed her arms over her ample bosom. She wore jeans, like Mary O'Mara, but hers were much tighter. Though she sported a man's button-front shirt, the fasteners at her chest were no match for her voluptuousness, and had popped open. Glimpses of a red bra peeked from a gap in the cotton plaid. "So this is that bad boy we've been hearing about." Whatever she'd been stirring with that wooden spoon was the color of tomato paste. A drop separated itself from the runny coating and spattered to the pine floor.

"Pauline, you're dripping." Mary pointed to the spoon.

The blonde continued to stare at Taggart, her expression designing. "Well, pardon me, but he's the cutest thing that's come into this kitchen in a long time."

Taggart was startled by the woman's unsubtle sexual overtures.

"For heaven's sake, Pauline." Mary stood at the sink where she'd apparently been getting a drink of water. She plunked down the tumbler, still half full, and walked across the kitchen to the cook. Her profile and demeanor were stiff, and she ignored Taggart with stanch determination. Taking the wooden spoon from the smirking blonde, she placed it on the spoon rest. "You're dripping spaghetti sauce."

The cook glanced at the floor. "Oops." She shrugged, which only served to widen the breach in her shirt.

"Pauline!" Mary said in a half whisper as she cast a severe look in Taggart's direction. "You're undone." She swiftly refastened the derelict buttons. "I'll be in the basement if you need me."

"Thanks, Mom." Pauline fixed her gaze on Taggart.

Mary disappeared out the back of the kitchen into an alcove that looked like it led to a rear porch. The stairs to the basement must be there, too, but Taggart couldn't see from his vantage point. All he knew was, even detesting him— *rather Bonn*—as Mary O'Mara did, her presence electrified a room. The loss of it made everything seem drab.

"Not to toot another woman's horn, but I've never seen Mary so—so…" She scrunched up her face, snarled and made clawing gestures.

Taggart's glance returned to Pauline. "So totally smitten?" he suggested sarcastically.

The cook looked momentarily confused, then laughed. "Yeah." She smoothed back a blond wisp that had fallen from her casually swirled and clipped hair. "When Mary can afford it, she takes night school courses to become a nurse. And nurses are supposed to get along with sick people—*crabby* sick people. I always thought she was pretty easygoing. Until you came along, that is."

So, Mary O'Mara could get along with any-body, except the one man she knew to be a self-centered playboy named Bonner Wittering. "Maybe she'd like me better if I came down with something," he suggested, adding silently, *preferably the Black Plague.*

The cook laughed again. "You're funny." She winked. "Funny and cute. I like that in a man."

He cleared his throat, uncomfortable with the direction of the conversation. He'd known other women like Pauline and sensed she was terribly insecure, at least where men were concerned. Through her wanton behavior, she was overcompensating, trying for "sex-kitten" but, instead, becoming a caricature.

She crossed the kitchen, holding out a hand. "I don't think we've been officially introduced. I'm Pauline Bordo. Miz Witty and Ruby call me Cook, which I hate." She winked again. "You can call me anytime."

Bearing in mind her feelings of inadequacy, he forced himself to remain civil and accepted her hand. "I'm—Bonn."

"Well, I *know* that. Everybody in town knows you're here."

Oh, great! Taggart grumbled inwardly. Bonn's reputation had certainly preceded him. So far he'd experienced four very different attitudes—suspicion, devotion, loathing and, now, lust. He wasn't sure he wanted to find out which dominated.

Glancing around he spotted the coffeemaker. Luckily it was half full. He indicated it with a nod. "I'm here for coffee. Miz Witty's waiting for me."

Pauline didn't release his hand. "That's too bad." She shifted a shoulder toward the bubbling sauce on the stove. "I'm not a live-in like Ruby and Mary, so I'm usually free by seven." She lifted her other hand and held his with both of hers. "Most nights I'm all dated up, but you whistle, handsome, and I'll come runnin'. I've heard a lot about you."

Apparently nothing high-minded or saintly, he responded mentally. "I'll keep your offer in mind." He disengaged himself from her two-fisted grip, headed to the coffeepot, grabbed a mug from the shelf above, and made quick work of pouring coffee. The whole time he felt her eyes on him. When he turned she was exactly where he'd left her.

She grinned. "Nice butt."

He supposed he shouldn't have been surprised by the comment, but he was. Barely containing his exasperation, he reminded himself she needed approval badly, poor thing. He would be polite if it killed him, but he would give her no hope of a romance in either word or deed.

Even so, he was supposed to be Bonner Wittering, the womanizing playboy. For the ruse to ring true he had to be somewhat glib. Without smiling, he lifted his coffee mug in a mock salute. "If I only had a dime for every time I've heard that."

Her wicked laughter was bold, a lusty invitation. Even if he had been the charred tree stump Mary O'Mara made him feel like, he couldn't have missed the fact that Pauline Bordo had a fixation on the "playboy" label that was part of the town's folklore about their most infamous native son.

She planted her fists on her hips causing one of the shirt button that Mary had fastened to pop open. He wondered if she practiced that move to be able to undo buttons on demand. "You surprise me, handsome."

Today hadn't been one of his best, and except for meeting Miz Witty, it was getting worse by the minute. Working to retain his polite facade, he glanced at the door and took a step in that direction. "I surprise you?" he repeated.

She must have nodded, since he didn't hear a response. "I figured I'd pitch and you'd catch, if you get my drift."

He did. She was about as subtle as her red underwear. He felt a headache coming on and wouldn't be surprised if the veins in his forehead were standing out like cords. He glanced in her direction.

"I've been pitching like a major leaguer, and you stand there like some cool-as-a-cucumber prince doing nothing but holding a cup of coffee." She smiled slyly. "I have to hand it to you big city playboys. You really know how to play a fish!" She winked again. She'd done it so often in the past five minutes, it was beginning to look like a facial tic. "Okay, pretty man, I'll play along. That smoldering I-don't-care act of yours is makin' me *hot!*"

She'd pegged the I-don't-care part, but *smoldering?* Taggart had a hard time suppressing his irritation. He felt sorry for her, but there was a limit. Striding toward the exit, he quipped, "Then my job here is done."

Pauline's lusty guffaws trailed him down the hall.

Taggart hadn't realized he'd fallen asleep until the melodious warble of his cell phone woke him. Groggy, he fumbled in the darkness for the bedside table. After grabbing his travel alarm, then his billfold, he blundered into his cell. Flipping it open, he muttered, "Lancaster."

"*Wrong,* Tag, old man. You're not supposed to be using your real name," came the familiar voice on the other end. "I hope nobody's sleeping with you."

Taggart couldn't mistake Bonn's voice. He rubbed his eyes and yawned. "Just the usual, a couple of supermodels."

"Slow day?"

Taggart was strung tight, but Bonn's joke had an effect. Even as aggravated as he was, he grunted out a half chuckle. "Maybe a little slow for Bonner Wittering, but I'm only pretending to be you. Why in Hades are you calling me at…" He squinted at the fluorescent dial on his travel alarm. "Nearly one-thirty in the morning? It must be, what? Almost three-thirty there?" He had a horrible thought and drew up on one elbow. "Tell me you're not in jail!"

Bonner's laughter rang through the phone. "Stop being an old woman. I'm a regular choir-boy, sitting here in my condo watching a fascinating infomercial. Did you know you can buy a belt with electrodes that will exercise your abs while you sleep?"

Taggart didn't need this right now. "Great. Order one and go to bed."

Bonn laughed, his unquenchable good nature magically taking Taggart's annoyance down another notch. "Okay, okay, I'll get to the point," he said. "I just wondered how it's going. When you didn't call, I decided I'd better check on you—see if they'd strung you up."

Taggart swung his legs over the side of the bed and sat up. "I'm still breathing. But I have a feeling Mary O'Mara has a hanging on her agenda."

There was a pause. "She's an old busybody with a bad attitude. Ignore her."

Taggart ran a hand through his hair. "Why didn't I think of that?"

Another pause. "I know it'll be hard, with her right there underfoot."

"Yeah. That, too," Taggart muttered, pushing the memory of a pair of smoke-gray eyes from his mind.

"Huh?"

"Nothing."

"Well, tell me about ol' Miz Witty. She swallowed it, right? Hook, line and sinker?"

"I guess so." Taggart hunched forward, resting a forearm on his thigh. "She's not very deaf or blind. Was that your embroidery or Miss O'Mara's?"

Another pause. "Miss? Is she a Miss?" Bonn asked, sounding like his playboy antenna was up and operational. "Is she pretty? Nah, probably one of those hateful, old-maid-types, right?"

Here we go again! "Try to focus, Bonn," Taggart said, pained at the reminder of how very pretty—and, as far as he was concerned—hateful, she was. "Did you lie about the deaf and blind thing or was it Mary?"

"Okay, okay. Let's see. I guess—maybe a little of both." He chuckled, sounding sheepish. "You know my motto: life's no fun if you can't embellish."

Taggart wished he could reach through the phone and throttle his friend, but he fought the urge. "You're damn lucky it's been a long time since she's seen you."

"But she really is sick, right? Mary told me she'd had a couple of strokes, and something else. I forget."

"Pneumonia. She can't walk, due to the strokes, but she seems to be on the mend. I'm no doctor, but she doesn't look like a woman on her death bed. Personally, I'm glad, because she's a nice lady." He paused, then decided he had to add, "You're a dirtbag for the way you've treated her."

"Look, I know that," Bonn said, sounding contrite. "I'm trying to make up for it, aren't I?"

Taggart frowned, took the phone from his ear and stared at it, astonished at Bonn's view of the situation. When he put the phone back to his ear, he grumbled, "*You* are sitting in your Boston condominium watching an infomercial about an electric belt. *I* am in Colorado, trying to make it up to her."

"Sure, sure. You're right," Bonn said. "You're doing—a lot. And I love you for it, bro." His apologetic tone sounded sincere. "Remember, it's her seventy-fifth birthday. That's a milestone. She *is* in fragile health, and I *am* stuck here, a slave to my bail bondsman. None of that's a lie. What you're doing is above and beyond the call."

"Yes, it is." Taggart needed sleep, and didn't want to start the same shopworn lecture over again, but by now it was such a reflex, he found himself saying, "You've got to start giving more thought to the consequences of your actions, Bonn, *before* you plunge in. If you'd only—"

The long, theatrical yawn he heard made Bonn's boredom clear. "Yeah, yeah. I'm reading you loud and clear, Tag." A pause. "Whoa, a new infomercial just started. Looks good. Something to do with women's thighs—"

"Go to bed!" Taggart cut in. "And don't call in the middle of the night for updates. If news of my murder doesn't show up in the national headlines, assume I'm okay. Remember the adage, 'No news is good news.'" He snapped shut the phone and tossed it aside. "I hope that goes for you, too, Bonn," he muttered, lying back.

Wide awake now, he laced his fingers beneath his head and stared into the darkness. He worried that infomercials about electric belts and thigh exercisers wouldn't hold Bonn's interest for long. He hoped his oldest friend would use his head for something beside scaffolding for the latest designer sunglasses.

Even as rash and immature as Bonn was, Taggart couldn't picture his life without him. Sure he had his faults, but he was an eternal optimist, always laughing, generous to a fault.

Taggart threw an arm over his eyes, vivid pictures of the long past flashing into his mind. Visions of himself and Bonn spooled by, as they were at the age of nine when they'd been thrown together by happenstance.

Taggart had been sent away to the Swiss boarding school when his parents died in a freak bridge collapse. His guardian and only relative was a crotchety, seventy-year-old great-uncle, a United States Supreme Court Justice, who smelled of stale cigars and old paper. Justice Lancaster might have been a great legal mind, but he didn't have the wherewithal to take in an orphaned child. Bonn, on the other hand, had been sent away because his parents couldn't deal with their imaginative, uninhibited, prankster son who refused to conform to his father's rigid, humorless temperament.

So, as young boys, Bonn and Taggart bonded in their loneliness. Taggart was Bonn's strength and Bonn was Taggart's exuberance. Bonn had always been able to make Taggart laugh, one of the few people who could. Being left alone at the remote school when the other boys went home for vacations and holiday breaks, Taggart was grateful for a friend who could bring humor to their abandonment. That's why he had never minded Bonn leaning on him.

Now they were both thirty-five, and Bonn was still leaning, not only as his longtime friend, but also as a legal client. After so many years, Taggart had to admit if only to himself, it was starting to wear thin. Taggart knew always being there to snatch Bonn out of the frying pan before he got burned wasn't helping him be a man, responsible for his own actions. The sad fact was, Bonn was an expert at manipulating Taggart with his humor and poor-pitiful-me act. Not to mention the inescapable *coup de grace,* when he reminded Taggart just *who* had introduced him to Annalisa, the love of his life.

Taggart experienced a gut punch of grief at the memory of his adored wife, lost five years ago in a fire at the hospital where she had been a pediatric surgeon. He still owed Bonn more than he could ever pay for Annalisa alone. Had it not been for his friend's impulsiveness, making plans with both Taggart and Annalisa that fateful evening, then forgetting them, running off to New York on a whim as they waited at his apartment door,

Taggart would never have met Annalisa. He wouldn't now have the precious memory of three blissful years loving her.

Unable to deny the fact that for all the rest of his days he would owe Bonn for giving him Annalisa, here Taggart was, in the small Rocky Mountain town of Wittering, for nearly two weeks—pretending to be someone he wasn't.

Taggart had been aware for some time that Miz Witty's caregiver had been writing to Bonn, trying to shame him into a visit. For some reason her last letter managed to make him see the error of his ways. Unfortunately, fate had Bonn hip-deep in another brush with Boston's legal system. This time it wasn't the usual small stuff, like the time he hired the marimba band to serenade his latest girlfriend at three in the morning, getting him arrested for disturbing the peace. This time his trouble wasn't simply an abundance of parking tickets or the occasional fistfight over a football team or a woman.

This time Bonn was implicated in a serious insider trading deal. Taggart felt sure Bonn had not meant to do anything criminal. His characteristic rashness and gullibility were at fault. Nevertheless, a trial date was set for late September, two months from now, and could end in serious jail time.

He lay there, his mind congested with the weight of the responsibility to save Bonn from his own foolishness, mixed with resentment at his friend for what they both were doing to Miz Witty.

With a low groan, he rolled to his stomach, any expectation of sleep he'd harbored proving to be crazed, wishful thinking.

Mary hadn't slept well. Her loathing for Bonner Wittering kept her tossing and turning all night. Just having that self-seeking rat in the house made her skin crawl. She felt sick to her stomach knowing the only way she had finally, *finally* managed to get him to come to Wittering was to hint that his grandmother was considering writing him out of her will.

What a sleaze! Telling him about her strokes, her heart and her pneumonia hadn't budged him, so she'd been forced to lie, big time. Mary was aware that Bonn had been writing to his grandmother for money. Apparently he'd nearly run through his own inheritance and started sweet-talking softhearted Miz Witty into paying for big chunks of his spendthrift lifestyle.

When Mary accidentally stumbled across one of Bonn's letters wheedling his grandmother for money, she'd known exactly what she would need to do to get him to visit—threaten him with The

Will. It had worked. He'd flown out so fast her head still spun. And because her ploy worked so swiftly, making it clear Bonn cared more about his finances than his grandmother's health, she despised him all the more.

Dragging herself up to sit, she stretched and yawned. Her glance fell on the framed picture on her bedside table. Even in her emotional turmoil, she managed a smile, kissed the tip of her finger and touched the face of her five-year-old, half sister Becca, a morning ritual, a silent prayer of sorts, thrown up to heaven. Mary's fondest wish was that somehow, by some miracle, she could wrestle custody of Becca away from the child's good-for-nothing father.

Sadly, miracles were hard to come by. Her spirits dipping again, she threw her legs over the side of the bed and stood, groggily pulling on her terry robe. She cinched up the sash and winced. What was she trying to do, slice herself in half? Loosening the belt, she stepped into her bedroom slippers and shuffled toward the bath. She heard water running. Ruby was up. Mary could always hear the water flowing through the pipes from the housekeeper's attic bathroom, above hers.

Movement caught her eye and she shifted to glance toward the rustic pine dressing table, her reflection in the wavy mirror glowered back at her. She instinctively ran both hands through her tousled hair. She narrowed her eyes, then shuffled closer. "Are those dark circles under your eyes?" she muttered. They were! "Drat you, Bonner Wittering!" She shifted away from the bedraggled sight, opened her mouth to express an additional thought, then changed her mind. She would not voice a notion that was so wayward and irrelevant—that Bonner Wittering had no business being as handsome as he was.

She remembered her first impression, in Miz Witty's room, when he'd turned to look at her. She'd been so dumbstruck she'd almost dropped the tray. His hawklike features were classically handsome, cunningly dramatic.

It was as though he knew just how to tilt his head, and organize his expression to appear slightly curious, vaguely troubled. She hated Bonn Wittering, yet her heart had taken a wild, mutinous leap of attraction. What did the man do, practice that look in front of a mirror to become just seductive enough—yet sincere enough—to dazzle and confuse the pants off a woman? She shook herself, not happy with the wording of that last thought.

Her reaction yesterday had been out of the blue, and it made her mad. When she'd lashed out at him at the top of the stairs she'd been as furious with herself as she was with him.

All night she'd struggled with her unwanted attraction for such an unworthy, self-centered jerk. This morning, she was adamant the sleepless hours had been well spent, exorcising the lewd demons from her body. She had trampled the worrisome delusion to dust. She might be exhausted, but she was back to loathing him with every sizzling, throbbing corpuscle of her being. She only hoped she would be able to avoid him for much of his stay. The idea of the need to smile at him and call him "Bonn" in any tone less than out-and-out revulsion was too painful to contemplate.

Her mind roved unaccountably to his eyes, the color of rich earth, framed by thick, dark lashes. They had been amazingly clear and candid, for a greedy, womanizing pig. But she supposed that's how greedy, womanizing pigs were able to womanize. They could look like nice guys with nothing but the most honorable intentions. That's what made them so dangerous!

She shoved open the bathroom door and froze, her body reacting before her mind grasped the truth. Standing there not two feet away, was the greedy, womanizing pig, himself—wearing nothing but a towel. Or maybe she should say, thank heaven he wore a towel!

Shaving cream covered one cheek and part of his jaw. As she stood there gripped by a bizarre paralysis, he stopped shaving and glanced her way. He didn't appear shocked. Possibly a little surprised. But then womanizing pigs were no doubt accustomed to having women burst into their bathrooms.

Lowering the razor to water running in the sink, he returned his attention to what he was doing. "Good morning, Miss O'Mara."

Lord, she'd forgotten both their bedrooms connected to the adjoining bath. Evidently she wasn't as alert this morning as she should be. Unfortunately, it was all his fault! "Oh—I'm..." She couldn't seem to form a coherent thought. For an out-and-out rat, he had a disturbingly masculine chest. So disturbing it could apparently rob women of the ability to think straight or even move. "I thought—I didn't think..." *Well, did you or didn't you, nitwit? Get hold of yourself!* She swallowed. "It's six o'clock. I didn't think you'd be up." *Get out. Close the door! What are you doing, planted in the doorway like a stupid pine tree?*

He lifted his chin and shaved upward along his jaw. "Actually, I slept late." He glanced her way as he rinsed the razor. "It's eight o'clock in Boston."

That surprised her. "I thought playboys slept till noon."

"And you're an expert on playboy behavior?"

Though she was having trouble getting her body to obey her, she worked on her stern expression. "Actually, my experience with playboys is limited to you," she said. "Naturally, I've heard of your..." She groped for a single word that would encompass the disreputable rumors over the years, about his sexual delinquency and general wild living. "...*exploits,*" she said finally. "You must know the topic of Bonner Wittering would be popular gossip in a town bearing his name." She paused, giving him a chance to respond. He merely carried on with his shaving. Annoyed by his disinclination to explain himself or at the very least express regret for his disgraceful behavior, she added, "However, it's been these past two years, getting to know you through your letters, that my low opinion of playboys has been set in stone."

"So, you judge all playboys by your estimation of me?" he asked, glancing her way.

She managed a shrug, gratified she could move her shoulders. She hoped the performance looked like utter indifference to his nearness. "Let's just say getting to know you has ruined me for all other playboys."

His lips twitched. "Why Miss O'Mara, are you flirting with me?"

She gasped. He was an incorrigible tease. "I'd rather cut off an arm!"

He broke eye contact and returned his attention to the mirror. "So, it's not really playboys you hate," he murmured. "It's me."

"If you're an example of what constitutes a playboy, then it's safe to say I'm not a fan of you—or *any* of your breed! Is that clear enough?"

"It seems fairly clear," he said. After a pause, he added, "I'll be out of your way in a minute."

Somehow, she regained the use of her arms and jerkily indicated the sink. "I—was just going to brush my teeth." *Why did you tell him that? What does he care? Get—out—of—the—room!*

He shifted his attention back to her. She wondered what was going through his mind. Nothing in his expression gave away his thoughts. He took a step back and indicated the sink with his razor. "Go ahead. I can see over your head."

She stared, realizing after a half dozen precariously rapid heartbeats her jaw had dropped and her mouth was open. Did he really think she'd get in front of him and bend over the sink—with him wearing nothing but a towel?

He lifted his chin and began to shave again. "Go ahead, Miss O'Mara." His lids slid to half mast, a clear indication he'd taken his eyes off the mirror and was watching her. "In case you're worried, the Playboy Handbook expressly prohibits attacking women in the act of brushing their teeth.''

She winced slightly as if her flesh had been nipped. Did this guy read minds?

''Pretend I'm not even here.'' As he dragged his razor across his cheek she thought she saw a muscle bulge there. Did it annoy him that she'd think he might attack her? Or did it bother him that she was probably not going to be a conquest.

Probably not? That didn't sound like she was sure about it! She shook herself. *Get with the program, Mary. You hate this man.* She saw him standing there, heard him when he spoke, yet she didn't see him, didn't hear him. Her thoughts ebbed and flowed as though she were slipping in and out of consciousness.

Before she grasped what was happening, he doused his razor under running water, replaced it on the glass shelf below the mirror and rinsed his face. He took a bottle of aftershave off the shelf, spattered it into his palm, rubbed his hands together and splashed the aromatic liquid on his cheeks and square jaw. She watched, transfixed, experiencing the kindling of an odd yearning deep inside her. For what? Certainly not this—this sexy— *No! No! I didn't mean sexy, I meant selfish! This selfish reptile.*

He replaced the cap on the bottle and set it aside then snagged her gaze. ''It's all yours, Miss

O'Mara.'' She stood there motionless, torn between wanting to look deeply into those hypnotic eyes and scratching them out. ''I'll just slither quietly away,'' he said, with the vaguest hint of a bow.

After he left, Mary didn't know how long she stood there, stock-still, trying to gather her fragmented thoughts. The bracing, woodsy scent of his aftershave lingered, turning her malfunctioning mind to slush.

After what seemed like an eternity she found herself able to move, and leaned heavily against the doorjamb. She ran her hands through her hair and grasped wads in her fists, furious for allowing herself to get—flustered. Yes, that was all it was. She'd been flustered. She hadn't expected to see him, especially nearly naked. The situation had been embarrassing and—and flustering.

She inhaled several deep breaths for strength, reminding herself of what she knew better than her own name. The man was a human slug. ''I hate you Bonner Wittering,'' she whispered in a guttural snarl. ''I will hate you until the end of time!''

CHAPTER THREE

TAGGART felt eligible for the Olympic Speed Eating race. One minute and twelve seconds had to be a record for consuming a stack of pancakes, a slab of ham, a tumbler of orange juice and a cup of coffee, which scalded the back of his throat.

The throat-scalding and the breakfast-bolting had been accomplished in a good cause. Otherwise, he might have found himself clasped in the embrace of the infatuated cook. Though aggravated and losing patience, Taggart was determined to remain sympathetic to Pauline's brazen overcompensations for her feelings of inadequacy.

He'd managed to break free of her panting attentions for a temper-cooling stroll through the evergreen forest behind Miz Witty's home, a shady cloister of low-growing pinyon pine, juniper, oak and towering ponderosas.

His hike over the rocky, forested landscape took him constantly upward. With every step he managed to rid himself of a little pent-up tension. He spotted a porcupine, a red fox and a mother deer with her fawn before emerging from the chill of the wood into a sun-drenched meadow. A clear, shallow brook meandered across the clearing, gurgling and sparkling in the sunshine for a dozen yards before tumbling back into the forest.

Beyond the meadow, past a steep chasm, the landscape was forbidding, yet stunningly beautiful, the earth, fractured and jagged. The timbered mountainside rising above the canyon was strewn with abandoned mining structures, no doubt part of the Wittering silver mining heritage. From what Bonn had told him over the years, savvy investing by several generations of Witterings, had multiplied the family's wealth a hundredfold, allowing Bonn the existence of leisure and excess he lived.

That thought brought Taggart harshly back to the present and the reason he was here. Spotting an outcropping of rock among a stand of tall ferns at the edge of the wood, he leapt across the shallow brook, walked to the boulder and sat down.

He scanned the clearing, awash with midmorning sunshine. Masses of flowers bobbed in the stony field, giving a delicate blue-violet cast to patches of ground. Along the bubbling stream, dense colonies of taller, pale pink flowers held court.

He inhaled crisp, clean air, experiencing a sense of peace in the vast quiet. He couldn't imagine why Bonn avoided his hometown with such a vengeance. Of course, Boston had a great deal to offer in convenience and comfort as well as historical significance, but this untouched wilderness held a grandeur far superior to mere convenience and creature comfort. Plus, its historical significance went back not merely a few hundred years, but eons.

He scanned the unbounded, cloudless sky. In this lofty realm a man could easily feel like Zeus himself, his thunderbolts cast aside, unnecessary amid such serenity. Truly, this sanctuary in the sky seemed too idyllic for mere mortals. He had the strangest sensation he'd been given a gift, just being allowed entry.

For the first time since arriving in Wittering, he didn't feel resentful. How many times in his life had he truly felt serene? Certainly never in his high-powered, litigious career. He sat very still for a long time, drinking in the quiet, becoming one with the solitude. He felt like a man who had been lost in a desert, dying of thirst, then stumbling into an oasis awash with cool, life-giving water. The single difference between Taggart and that tragic wayfarer was that Taggart hadn't been aware of the depth and breadth of the parched void inside him.

The realization was both shocking and compelling, sending his conflicting emotions into a bitter fight for supremacy. He told himself his life was exciting, filled with challenges. He had power, respect, money—was a big fish in a big pond. So, why then did he find being in this quiet spot on a remote mountain so significant, so potent, it made him doubt everything he was?

It's the prehistoric cave dweller in you talking, his logical side insisted. Sure, it was tempting, this idea of getting away from everything. But it was a pipe dream. A man had to survive in the *real* world, make a living. "Hell," he muttered, "Getting away from the rat race is what vacations are for." He wasn't sure he appreciated his term "rat race" but, since he'd been the one to think it, he let it pass without examination. Nobody's job was perfect. Cave dwellers had to risk life and limb just to eat.

As careers went, his was as vital as it was profitable. His quandary, this unexpected emotional quagmire, was simple to explain. He was sleep-deprived, and a little disoriented—thrust into the position of suddenly being so loved, so loathed and so lusted after, all in one day. That could be hard on any man's psyche.

He heard rustling and turned expecting to find another mother deer with her baby, or a fox, maybe an elk. Instead, he was astonished to see a being far more extraordinary, exotic and welcome, no matter how unwelcoming her reaction might be when she noticed him.

Her back to him, she walked along the edge of the brook as it took a turn into the sunny meadow. Spilling over the crook of her arm, an array of willowy, blue flower clusters bobbed with her every step. She knelt to pick a handful of the tall, pink flowers at the stream's edge. Her dark hair fluttered and cavorted in the breeze, taunting him with come-ons he knew to be lies.

She rose, the move as graceful as any prima ballerina. Wearing hiking boots, jeans and a clingy, white turtleneck, she walked on. In full, bright sunlight, she paused before a bush, a riot of contrast with light green leaves and bright red berries. Using garden shears she snipped off several branches and added them to her bouquet.

Some of the flowers she carried were identical to those in the vase in his room. He'd seen several others he'd recognized in the plantings around the house. It hadn't occurred to him that anyone would hike up a mountainside to gather wild-flowers, simply to decorate a home.

What an urban creature he'd become. Or was it more likely his status as a widower? Before Annalisa's death, she had insisted on having fresh flowers in the house, year-round. They'd come from a Boston florist, not a mountain meadow, but those bouquets had been one of the subtle feminine touches in life he'd lost with his wife's death. He'd stuffed the memories into a dark corner of his mind as he'd thrown himself into his law practice, his way of dealing with his grief. He experienced a melancholy jab at that realization. He didn't want to forget, yet remembering held its own kind of pain.

Mary O'Mara seemed to be having trouble juggling her swelling bouquet and snipping the berry laden branches at the same time. As he watched, she dropped her gardening shears. He decided to quit feeling sorry for himself and be useful. He planned to offer her help, no matter how much she loathed him. He stood, recalling this morning when she'd barged into the bathroom, obviously not expecting to find him there.

She'd been horrified, aghast, dumbfounded—however he cared to label it, she had been far from happy. Even in her abhorrence, she'd been a stirring sight, her hair in charming disarray, her cheeks bright pink with shock and embarrassment. Her smoke-gray eyes dazzling, even glittering with antipathy.

She had such a troubling, gut-level effect on him, the sight of her standing there had been hard to deal with. It had taken every ounce of control not to slice off his nose. He'd known this trip would be two difficult weeks, but he hadn't counted on the likes of Mary O'Mara, making his sticky situation one hell of a lot stickier.

He loved Annalisa and always would. This surprising attraction to Mary was hard to understand. He didn't want to feel stirrings for another woman. When his wife died, he'd contented himself with the fact that he'd had his great love, been luckier than most men. Then Mary walked into his life. The beauty of the experience had been pure, blinding and profound. Her forced smile and white-hot hatred hadn't dimmed or sullied its significance. He didn't understand it, was bewildered by it, and tried to put it out of his mind.

He had enough to contend with right now. First, he wasn't Bonn Wittering. And second, even if he were open to love, he couldn't tell Mary the truth about who he was. She would be furious with the deceit and refuse to go along with lying to Miz Witty. He had no doubt that she would immediately inform her employer, and in the process break the elderly woman's heart. In Mary's position, he would probably do the same thing.

This troubling, uninvited attraction he felt for Miz Witty's caregiver had to be ignored, killed. The deception had begun and must proceed as planned. He headed down the slope toward the brook, hiking up the sleeves of his beige v-neck shirt. Getting into character as the carefree Bonner Wittering, he called, ''Need any help?''

Her body jerked at the sound of his voice, as though she'd been stung by a wasp. He heard her startled gasp. She spun around. Her eyes wide, she scanned the distance, quickly zeroing in on him. *''You!''* She closed her eyes for a split second, as though gathering her poise, then glared. ''You scared the life out of me! What are you doing skulking around here?''

His hiking boots were waterproof so he waded through the shallow brook to where she stood. ''I was looking around.'' Bonn had undoubtedly seen all this as a child, so he added, ''You know—for old times' sake?'' He indicated her burden. ''Why don't I hold those while you cut?''

She looked down at her bouquet and frowned, as though the idea of Bonn Wittering touching the flowers would contaminate them to the point where they'd wither and turn to dust. Her obvious disinclination to have him pollute her bouquet annoyed him, but he hid his feelings and knelt to retrieve her shears. ''Or I could do the cutting. Just tell me what you want.''

She sucked in a quick breath, then exhaled as quickly. ''Okay, I'd appreciate it very much if you'd go to Hades.''

He grunted a cynical chuckle. He'd laid himself wide open for that one. "Yeah, well—besides that."

Her glance shifted to the shears he held, then to her armload of flowers. After a brief pause, she said, "I think I have enough." She held out her hand. "Give me the shears. I need to get back to the house."

He noticed her focus was on his neck, not his face. "No problem, Miss O'Mara." He stuffed the gardening shears in the front, right pocket of his jeans. "I'm on my way back, and you've got enough to carry."

Her glance flicked to his eyes. He could tell she was dismayed that he'd deposited the shears where she couldn't get at them—unless she dived into his pants. He knew she'd rather be swallowed whole by a bear.

"Shall we go?" He took her arm.

She yanked away from his touch. "You have *got* to be kidding!"

He wasn't surprised by her rejection and tried to tell himself he didn't care. "Look, even a neglectful grandson can be a gentleman," he said.

"Well, be one someplace else. If you'll recall, Mr. Wittering, I told you to stay away from me."

"If you'll recall, Miss O'Mara," he countered, "I don't always do what I'm told."

That remark got him a fiery glare. "You *would* brag about it!" She turned her back and stomped downhill toward the shady wood.

Taggart could tell she was determined to put distance between them. *You can try to get away,* he told her silently. *But unless you break into a full run, you're out of luck.* He was quite a bit taller than she, his legs longer, making his stride impossible for her to outdistance as long as they were both walking. All through the forest, the ground was covered with pine needles and leaves, camouflaging potential hazards on the rock-strewn, uneven terrain. Running with her arms loaded down would be foolish.

He caught up to her in four easy strides. "What's that perfume you have on? It smells like vanilla." Actually he'd smelled it long before she arrived, but it was the only thing he could come up with at the moment besides the nagging question he hated wanting to ask. The one that went something like, *May I kiss you to see if it's as good as I think it would be?*

"Ponderosa pine," she said, her attention straight ahead. At least "Ponderosa Pine" is what he thought she said, since she'd spoken through thinned lips and gritted teeth.

"Pardon?" he asked, keeping his tone conversational.

"Sunshine makes their bark smell like vanilla."

"Oh." He watched her stern profile. "That's interesting."

She swerved around a lacy thicket of tall ferns. A winglike frond brushed one of the berry-laden branches off her bouquet. Either she didn't notice or she didn't plan to slow down enough to retrieve it. Taggart rescued it from the wagging frond. When he caught up with her he asked, "Are these berries poisonous?"

She glanced his way for a flash, then returned her attention to the maze of trees ahead. "Eat one and find out."

He couldn't repress a grin. "Okay."

He plucked off one of the berries and, after a brief delay, popped it in his mouth, trusting her hatred for him stopped short of homicide. He chewed, startled to find the fruit tasted like lemonade. "It's not bad."

She didn't respond.

"How long have I got before I keel over?"

She shifted to glower at him. "Sadly, they're perfectly harmless."

He found himself grinning again. "What a shame."

He lay the branch on top of her bouquet, and she gathered it into her arms along with the others. "I'd have thought you'd know that." She peered at him. "Having been born here."

He experienced a prick of apprehension but covered with a nonchalant shrug. "It's refreshing to discover you can be wrong."

She stared hard at him for a couple of steps, but the terrain wasn't the soft and gentle kind you could take your attention away from for too long without regretting it, so she snapped her focus forward.

"Remember, I was shipped off to boarding school at nine. A boy can forget a lot of details about a hometown he's hardly visited in over a quarter of a century."

"I'm sure!" she said. "Like the *detail* of his grandmother!"

He gave her a quick look, then returned his attention to the twisty trail. The mention of Miz Witty brought a question to his mind. "How is she today?"

"She's fine," Mary said, her tone clipped. "This is her bouquet. She's eating breakfast now. As soon as she's through she'll want to bathe. Then we'll do a little physical therapy for her leg." She glanced his way, her expression defiant. "She'll be ready for company about eleven."

He absorbed that news. "Then tell her I'll see her at eleven."

Mary's expression didn't ease. He sensed rather than saw her relief.

He shook his head, marveling that she could so completely and utterly distrust him. "What did you think I'd do, visit her one evening then ignore her?"

"I wouldn't put anything past you," she said.

He looked ahead, glimpsing the house through the trees, which brought on another thought. "Please inform Pauline that I'll be eating lunch with Miz Witty."

Mary peered at him, clearly dubious. Of course, she didn't know his problem with the oversexed cook. Even if he hadn't enjoyed Miz Witty's company, he would choose eating lunch with a pack of ravenous wolves over Pauline-the-winker.

"I usually eat lunch with Miz Witty," she said after a pause.

He was surprised, but didn't know why he should be. "I'll be joining you, then," he said, aware of the crimp that news put in her day.

She remained grimly mute as they hiked to the edge of the forest. The redwood steps leading to the back porch loomed ahead of them. Beyond that was the kitchen. Taggart had no intention of making that trip.

"Here." He retrieved the garden shears from his pocket and held them out. "I think I'll walk into town."

She halted, glanced at him. Her attention trailed from his face to his hand and the shears he lifted toward her. Without comment, she took them and resumed her trek toward the back door.

"Me, too," he said.

She stopped, turned, looking suspicious. "What?"

He crossed his arms over his chest, taunting, "I enjoyed our stroll, too." That would get a rise out of her.

Her eyes flashed and her cheeks reddened. "Mr. Wittering, we did not stroll, and whatever it was, I did not enjoy it." Snapping her shoulders around she broke into a run across the lawn. He felt sure she'd longed to do that from the beginning.

"I'll see you at lunch," he called, his reward a half-step falter in her stride and a definite stiffening of her spine.

As he watched her flee, he pondered his behavior. He was surprised at himself for teasing her. It wasn't like him. What obscure, insubordinate part of him was responsible for this aberrant behavior? Why was he teasing this woman— a woman who hated the man she believed him to be? What contrary force inside him was not only disregarding his own counsel to kill the attraction, but purposefully drawing out her passion in the form of hostility, simply to glimpse it?

He pivoted away to go around the house. Shaking his head at himself, he muttered, "What's wrong with you, Lancaster?"

Mary feared her lips would be permanently frozen in the strained smile she'd been compelled to wear during lunch with Miz Witty and Bonn Wittering. The only good thing about it had been her employer's delight. She looked ten years younger and happier than Mary had ever seen her. Which only made her desire to kick Bonn Wittering in the shins harder to resist. He'd been so careless of this wonderful woman's feelings for so long.

And his shins were so near! He sat directly across from her at the oak card table. It would be a crime not to kick him, just once. *Really hard.*

"I'll help clear the dishes." A voice intruded on her spiteful fantasy. A male voice. She glanced across the table, situated in front of Miz Witty's hearth. Mary had spent the last, endless hour confined there with Bonn and her boss, conversing over a meal of tuna salad, stuffed in a tomato, marinated asparagus tips, orange slices and hot tea. Mary had a feeling Bonn was accustomed to eating more for his midday meal, and felt a gush of satisfaction at that. Let him be hungry!

"Mary?" The man causing her so much stress stood up, aiming a painfully exhilarating smile her way.

She wondered if his face muscles were as tired from their farce as hers. "Yes?" she asked, continuing to pretend she didn't think he was the most self-centered man on earth.

"I said I'd help clear the table."

She nodded and placed her napkin beside her plate. "How—nice." She stood and moved to Miz Witty's side, affectionately squeezing her employer's hand. "Is there anything I can get you?"

Miz Witty beamed, her normally pale cheeks rosier than Mary had seen them in their two and-a-half years together, her eyes bright with contentment. "No dear. I'm going to read until tea time." She removed her hand from Mary's and patted the younger woman's face. "Tell Cook the lunch was delicious, as usual." She lowered her hands to the wheels of her wheelchair and began to back away from the table.

"May I help?"

Startled to hear the offer, Mary glanced at Bonn. He was certainly laying on the Sir Galahad act pretty thick! Why should she be surprised? Bonn Wittering had a lot to lose if his grandmother cut him out of her will. She was a wealthy woman, and Bonn was her only relative. If

Mary's suspicions were true, Bonn had run through his own inheritance and couldn't afford to alienate his grandmother. Mary had no doubt that was the real reason he'd finally come back to Wittering.

Miz Witty beamed at her grandson. "That's a very sweet offer, dear. If you wouldn't mind, I'd like to sit by the window. It's such a beautiful day." She pointed to her bedside table. "My book is over there."

Mary began to clear the table, working to ignore the man. She pursed her lips, gratified to know she could actually change her expression to one more suited to her real mood.

As she placed the last of the china and silverware on the serving tray, the man responsible for her grimness materialized beside her. "I'll take that."

Kick his shins now! she roared inwardly. But she knew she couldn't, not even if Miz Witty weren't in the room. Regretful, she stepped away and indicated the tray, piled with dirty dishes. Since her back was to Miz Witty she didn't smile. For show, she added a lighthearted lilt to her voice. "Why, thank you so much, Bonn." She gave him a look that shouted her desire to hurt him physically. The slight narrowing of his eyes told her he'd received her message.

He picked up the tray and walked toward the open bedroom door. Mary turned toward Miz Witty who watched them, smiling. The older woman waved her away. "Why don't you and Bonn go for a walk, have a nice long visit. I'm sure he'd enjoy the company of a lovely young woman."

Mary managed a grin, nodded at her employer but inwardly grumbled, *Over my dead body!* "What a—lovely idea." Exiting the room, Mary rolled her eyes, grateful Bonn had already left and couldn't have heard the detestable suggestion.

When Mary reached the bottom of the staircase, Bonn appeared so suddenly, they almost collided. He no longer held the tray. Taking a step back, she put distance between them. "You made quick work of leaving the dishes," she said.

He didn't smile. She couldn't tell if the serious expression was annoyance at her for moving away—some kind of playboy-ego thing—or if he was as weary as she, forced to sustain a fake smile from eleven in the morning until one in the afternoon. She didn't know why he should be weary of it. Womanizers surely had well-exercised smile muscles.

"Was I supposed to wash the dishes?" he asked.

She took another step back and found herself against the wall. She flattened herself there. "Uh—no. Pauline does the dishes."

He nodded, eyeing her quietly. Nervous flutterings pricked at her chest. She swallowed. Staring into warm, earth-brown eyes that had an uncanny ability to seem so—so earnest, was confusing and disorienting. She tried to look away but the hypnotic effect of his gaze short-circuited her ability, highly disconcerting.

She wasn't accustomed to feeling this strange, agitated dichotomy about people. About men. But this man confused, frustrated and disturbed her. She disliked him with all her heart, but the restless disquiet that tightened her chest wasn't dislike. She wished it were. It was an uneasiness without a name, and she didn't like it.

Finally, her nerves frayed and her breathing labored, she demanded hoarsely, "What are you looking at?"

Her fretful question furrowed his brow. He peered at her intently for another pair of heartbeats, then startled her by placing the flats of his hands on the wall on either side of her face. "Your lips," he murmured.

Mary didn't have time to react, or even to be sure she'd heard him right before his lips touched hers, then covered her mouth, making her senses spin. She experienced a lurch inside her, an unwelcome flood of excitement. His kiss was warm, slow and surprisingly gentle. Delicious sensations spiraled through her, heating the blood in her veins and making her heart pound.

His kiss didn't demand, it caressed. Didn't dominate, it delighted. His lips coaxed, pleasuring in their exploration. She felt transported on a soft and airy cloud as she drank in the honeyed sweetness.

He touched nothing but her mouth, yet that contact was so powerful her limbs grew numb. She felt drugged, couldn't move, though she wanted to lift her arms and encircle his neck, pull him close. She wanted to hold him, feel his heartbeat against her own. But she'd lost the capacity to do anything but quiver helplessly, thrilling as pleasure radiated through her.

"I'm sorry." His lips stroked hers erotically as he made the guttural apology—a taunting termination to his kiss. He pushed away from the wall. As he distanced himself, Mary could only stare, too dazed and breathless to react.

"Forgive me—I..." His voice hoarse, he shook his head, as though not sure what to say.

In the waiting silence she stared at his set features, clamped jaw and dark, seductive eyes. Blood pounded unmercifully in her head, making it hard to hear, hard to think. She tried to work up some indignation, but she couldn't. She'd never been kissed like that before. She'd never even dreamed of being kissed like that!

"It was wrong of me," he ground out. Looking tormented, he dragged a hand through his hair. "I don't suppose you'd believe me if I said I've never done anything like that before?"

She might not be hearing too well at the moment and she might not have all her faculties in tip-top condition, but she heard his question. And he was right. She didn't believe *that*. Telling her such a bold-faced lie, while managing to look irresistibly anguished and angry with himself, required a lot of talent—and, unquestionably, a great deal of experience!

Did this carousing Boston playboy think his "I've-never-done-anything-like-that-before" act would really work for a man with such a notorious reputation—no matter how skillfully played? Did he think because she was an unsophisticated, small town girl she'd be easy pickings?

The fact that she so obviously despised him made her a challenge. *A challenge!* To him, kissing her had been nothing but a careless and cruel game. To her, it had been a mind-blowing excursion into a realm of sensual perfection she wished she'd never encountered. Struggling to hold back tears she refused to let him see, she fought to conquer her anger and hurt.

Pushing away from the wall, she edged toward the entrance to the dining room and her escape to the kitchen. ''Who...'' she croaked. Clearing her throat, she forced steel into her words. ''Who am *I* to question *your* honesty?'' she jeered.

CHAPTER FOUR

TAGGART could not believe what he'd done. He'd actually kissed Mary O'Mara. Blindsided her. *And himself!* Naturally she wouldn't believe him when he said he'd never done anything like that before. After all, he was Bonner Whitney Wittering the Fourth, womanizing ne'er-do-well. At least he was as far as Wittering, Colorado was concerned.

Taggart eyed the dusty rose wall beside the staircase where, only a moment ago, he'd trapped Mary O'Mara's face between his hands. He couldn't get her shocked expression out of his head—her complexion winsomely high, eyes flashing with hostility and hurt. Why this woman? What was it about her that had the power to touch him at a level no other human being on earth had been able to reach—since Annalisa?

How different the two women were. Like night and day. Dr. Annalisa Wayne Lancaster, well-born pediatric surgeon, brilliant, sophisticated, ever gracious. Then, there was Mary O'Mara, nursemaid, a blunt, country girl who had probably never been farther from Wittering than Denver, just over an hour away by car.

Even so, the life flashing in her eyes fascinated and mesmerized him. The spirit and passion she exhibited in her devotion to Bonn's grandmother, impressed and inspired him. The women he'd dated since Annalisa's death had been from Boston society or highly educated professionals: doctors, professors, several executives, even one congresswoman.

Then there was Lee Stanton, a partner in his law firm. They'd had a six-month affair that had ended in early spring. He regretted getting involved with Lee, considering he had to see her at work every day. Especially since she refused to believe their affair was over.

None of these other women, with all their breeding and education, could compare to Mary O'Mara when it came to how she made him feel. He peered toward the front door, deciding he should make himself scarce for a while, give Mary some space. He headed outside onto the porch, angry with himself. ''Kissing her is no damn way to kill an attraction, idiot!'' he gritted out.

When it came to love, he'd fallen quick and hard. He'd been fortunate with Annalisa. She'd fallen quick and hard, too. All the others since his wife's death had meant nothing, just bouts of loneliness temporarily deflected. Not love. Never love. Never again. Annalisa's memory was too precious.

Hustling down the steps to the gravel drive, he muttered, "You were lucky in love once, my friend. Don't get greedy. You've kissed her. It's out of your system. Now move on." Unfortunately, he couldn't "move on" from Wittering for ten more days.

His mood grim, he thrust his hands in his pockets and strode down the serpentine, sloping drive to the blacktop road leading to town, an easy half-mile walk. He'd already been there once today. It was his own fault that he had no choice but to go again. He needed to move and keep moving. If things kept going the way they had so far on this trip, he would get to know the town intimately— out of necessity, to keep his distance from Mary O'Mara and her magnetic lips.

He heard the ding-ding of the approaching trolley's bell as it proceeded along its route around town. Taggart ignored it, ignored the people clustered at the trolley stop, and leapt across the tracks. He needed to walk or he would explode with fury at his impulsiveness. He'd behaved more like his rash, thrill-seeking friend and client, Bonn Wittering, than Taggart Jerod Lancaster. Ordinarily he was so careful, so adamant about preparing for any possibility before he acted, his law partners kiddingly referred to him as "The Boy Scout."

He blew out an exhale through gritted teeth. "You're an attorney, not a method actor!" he muttered, trekking downhill toward Wittering's main street. "Don't get carried away with the act."

He tried to get his mind off Mary and the kiss by taking in the scenery. Wittering was typical of many villages nestled in the Rockies, surrounded on all sides by snowcapped behemoths and accessible only by cliff-hugging highways that leap-frogged steep divides. His trek took him past quaint, century-old homes of painted siding and native stone, nestled side-by-side with contemporary stucco, redwood and log houses, one or two as new as the spring thaw.

A stack of condominiums was under construction, amid an evergreen thicket, the staccato sound of nail guns drowning out the high, wild scream of an eagle, the gentle babble of a tumbling creek and the whisper of wind through tall, skinny pines.

Further down, beyond the cascading homes, the structures became small businesses that spilled onto Center Street. A mile-long stretch of shops and homey restaurants, Wittering's main thoroughfare invited tourists and residents alike to enjoy their rustic, cozy ambience.

Taggart walked toward the main boulevard, paying little heed to the side street shops. Suddenly someone exited a store directly in front of him and he couldn't avoid a collision. In a mental flash, he realized he'd run into a woman, and she was falling. Instinctively, he grabbed her by the shoulders to halt her tumble. "I'm sorry," he said. "I should have been more care—"

The woman he'd collided with cleared long, dark hair out of her eyes and looked up at him. He could tell by the near-smile on her face she'd been about to say something like "No problem," or "I'm fine." But when she recognized him, her expression mutated into a glower. He released her, since the anger in her eyes made her desire to be free of his contaminating touch quite clear. After some brief, knife-sharp eye contact, she dropped her attention to the sidewalk. His gaze followed hers down to notice a package he'd obviously knocked from her hand. He bent to retrieve it just as she did, his fingers closing over hers.

"I have it," she said, in a tone that meant *"Don't touch me!"*

He let her go and straightened. "I'm sorry, Mary," he repeated, meaning it. "I didn't see you." He had no idea she would be in town. She must have dashed through the kitchen, out the back door, then struck out toward town in a dead run.

She straightened, making a production of checking the contents of her bag.

"Did I break anything?" he asked, wishing he could somehow make amends for the crazy kiss.

She shook her head, keeping her attention riveted on the bag and what was inside it. "I don't think so."

Self-reproach clung to him like a heavy overcoat. He couldn't erase the image of her shock and outrage over his irrational kiss. "Look," he said, "I can't apologize enough about—the other thing, too."

She stilled, one hand deep in the sack. She clearly hadn't expected him to bring that up.

"How can I make it up to you?" he asked.

She blinked, withdrew her arm and closed the plastic bag. "Forget it. Just—forget it."

"Could I buy you a cup of coffee?"

She peered his way, clutching the sack to her chest like a shield. "You don't seem to get it, Mr. Wittering," she said, her words slow and measured, as though trying to make it clear enough for even a moron to understand. "What you can do for me is—*stay out of my sight.*"

He experienced the prick of her statement even as his gaze was drawn to her mouth. That dangerous, seductive mouth. Her fuller lower lip perched erotically above a defiant, jutting chin. He noted that her upper lip was slightly slimmer, yet, together, in their serendipitous union, they embodied the perfect valentine.

Irresistible.

Looking at those lips now, he could almost forgive himself for his lapse. He'd never seen such a blatantly kissable mouth in his life.

"Did you hear what I said?" she asked, breaking into his wayward reverie. She apparently hadn't expected him to loiter there, watching her after she'd told him in no uncertain terms to go away.

He shook himself out of the trance her lips seemed able to draw him into. "Yes, I heard." That strange, renegade part of him took charge, adamant that she not leave and that he not walk away either. He searched around for a reason she might stay. Miz Witty's happiness and welfare seemed to be his best bet. "I need to ask a favor of you."

She stared, mutely. Her wide-eyed disbelief didn't surprise him. He was sure she assumed he would do as she demanded and get out of her sight. "You want to ask a favor of *me?*" she echoed after a long, stunned silence. The stupefaction in her voice was no great shock.

Sure, it took crust to ask a favor of her when she'd just told him she wanted nothing to do with him. What Mary O'Mara didn't know was that, as a trial lawyer, crust was part of the job description. He smiled wryly. "I know it's hard to believe."

"It's impossible to believe." She swallowed, looking as though keeping eye contact was torture. "Unless you'd like me to slap your face, which I admit would be a pleasure."

He couldn't help lifting a dubious brow in a wordless, sardonic response.

"I was afraid that wasn't it." She turned on her heel, presenting her back to him. "Goodbye."

"It's about Miz Witty."

When she skidded to a halt he knew his gamble had paid off. For Miz Witty, Mary O'Mara would stick her head in a lion's mouth. She shifted toward him, her expression distrustful and troubled. He didn't need clairvoyant powers to read her mind. She obviously feared she was head and shoulders inside the lion's mouth right now.

"What about Miz Witty?" she asked tightly.

He pushed up his sleeves, working to appear ultra-casual and harmless as a newborn lamb. No more surprise attacks. He planned to convey that silent promise in his nonassertive demeanor. Unfortunately, he didn't know how well he would succeed. For one thing, Mary's lips taunted him cruelly. Secondly, being a trial lawyer had drilled any nonassertive tendencies out of him years ago.

Third, and most disturbing, that traitorous and contrary entity so recently born in him, was in full control, overriding the logical, Boy Scout mentality that usually guided his behavior. He should be walking away by now! *Why the hell wasn't he?*

"It's Tuesday." He wore his most earnest, most trustworthy courthouse expression, the one he used when appealing to a jury to find his client "not guilty." "Miz Witty's birthday is Thursday, the twenty-fourth, and I haven't bought her gift." He lifted his hands in a gesture of helplessness, the image of a man out of his element when it came to shopping. "I wondered, since you know her so well, if you'd help me."

She didn't even try to hide her mental turmoil. He watched a gamut of emotions flicker in her eyes and could almost hear her internal scream of frustration. She stirred uneasily, shifted her shopping bag to under one arm. Her gaze skittered away and she readjusted her bag, then relocated the plastic sack to its shielding position, hugging it with both arms. "Well..." she said, her voice wavering. She coughed behind a fist. "Well, I suppose—for Miz Witty."

He felt like smiling but he didn't. He merely nodded. "I appreciate it." He indicated Center Street, half a block ahead. "That way?"

She nodded, keeping eye contact brief.

"What do you think she'd like?" he asked, adjusting his pace to her shorter stride.

Mary accompanied him toward the main street, clutching her bag to her breast. She couldn't have looked more unwilling if he'd been leading her to her own hanging. After a long, solemn interlude, she answered his question. "Miz Witty is not a woman who needs much to make her happy." She peered at him meaningfully. "A little attention goes a long way."

He met her gaze. "If it makes you happy to bludgeon me with reminders of my failings, go ahead. But just so you'll know, there's something to be said for subtlety."

She laughed, a short, sarcastic burst of sound. "Subtlety? *You?* I spent two whole years trying to get you here. If there's one thing I've learned in all that time, Mr. Wittering, it's that *subtlety* is wasted on you."

She had a point. As far as sensitivity was concerned, Bonn was like a bull in a china shop. The closest Taggart ever got to subtlety with Bonn consisted of grabbing him by the shirtfront and shouting, *"Listen to me, you idiot!"*

No doubt that was why she'd had to exaggerate Miz Witty's health crisis. "Well, you got me here. That's the important thing."

She blinked, looking strangely taken aback. Her eyes glittered, heralding a storm. "Yes, I did.'' She flicked her gaze ahead, her bearing stiff. He couldn't imagine what sparked the surge of renewed anger. Was she mad at herself for lying about Miz Witty's health? He'd expected her to be slightly shamefaced about that, if anything.

Apparently being reminded of his—Bonn's—negligence could set her off as quickly as striking a match. She obviously didn't feel guilty pangs for lying about Miz Witty's impending demise. To her, the means—in other words, a bold-faced lie—was justified by the end—getting a reluctant, self-centered grandson to visit.

He decided he'd better change the subject. Another few seconds of stewing and Mary would stomp off mad, her decision to help him tossed aside in the dust. ''What about a compact disc player and some disks?'' he suggested. ''I noticed she likes to have a radio on, and the reception is full of static.''

Mary's stern profile grew contemplative and she glanced his way. ''Yes. I think she'd like that.''

They stood on the corner of Center and Third. He indicated the main street with a broad gesture. ''Which way to the compact disc player store?''

''I think the mercantile.'' She indicated the way. ''I was going there anyway.''

As they strolled the town's main artery, the sun shone down on them, warm and restorative. The air, though thinner up here, smelled fresh. The trolley rumbled by. Street traffic was light. Only a handful of shoppers strolled along, laughing and talking. Several waved and called out friendly greetings to Mary. She responded with smiles and equally friendly replies. Taggart found himself trying to catch glimpses of her smiling. He shouldn't have tried. Mary, *really* smiling, did things to him, made the blood course through his veins like a Colorado river thawed by the sun's heat in springtime. This was *not* killing his attraction! Was he some kind of masochist?

"Mary, see you at the birthday party?" a husky, lumberjack type called out as he approached along the sidewalk.

"Sure Jake." She smiled and waved.

"I get the first dance, right?"

She laughed, the lilting sound causing Taggart's skin to prickle pleasantly, as though she'd run teasing fingertips over his bare flesh. "I wouldn't have it any other way."

As the young man passed them, his glance transferred to Taggart. The message he received was not neighborly. Taggart didn't know if the spiteful flash in Jake's gaze was because the townsfolk thought he was the infamous Bonn Wittering, or if any man lucky enough to walk with Mary O'Mara would reap killer glares from less fortunate males. Taggart nodded a curt greeting without offering a smile, either. Irrational as it was, he felt proprietary toward Mary.

The stranger's palpable antagonism toward Taggart made him take more notice of passersby. "There will be dancing at Miz Witty's party?" he asked.

"Yes. Miz Witty might not be able to dance, but she wants her guests to have fun." Her tone lacked friendly lightness now that she was once again speaking to him.

"I see." He supposed he could count on being elected President of the United States before Mary would agree to dance with him.

Taggart watched the faces of the men as they passed. On the whole they went about their business paying Taggart and Mary no particular heed, so he found himself relaxing. Most of Wittering's roving populous wore jeans, work shirts or T-shirts and hiking boots. Many of the men sported beards and the women wore little or no makeup, like Mary. These mountain dwellers were plain folk, hearty individualists. They put on no airs, harbored no hidden agendas, weren't driven incessantly to acquire the most toys and the power to choose the games. "I like Wittering," he said.

"You have a strange way of showing it."

He cursed inwardly at his lapse. How quickly he could forget. *He was supposed to be a native of this little burg!* He glanced at her and eased into a cynical, half smile. "I meant—in small doses."

"Like every quarter century or so?"

"Yeah." That was a lie. He really liked Wittering. He bet the population exploded in the wintertime, when skiers invaded. He'd loved skiing as a kid, but hadn't had the chance since leaving Switzerland, when he'd enrolled at Harvard. More like, he hadn't taken the time. "Or when my grandmother has a seventy-fifth birthday."

"That's sad." Mary shook her head at him. "You're really something, you know it?"

He frowned, baffled. "What do you mean?"

There was almost an imperceptible note of pleading in her expression. "You're saying you won't be back."

He realized what she meant. When he left town Miz Witty would once again be deserted by her one and only relative. He didn't know how to respond. After all, he wasn't Bonn Wittering, and heaven only knew whether Bonn could ever come back, even if he wanted to. His trial would determine whether he'd spend the next decade in prison. Taggart decided to defuse the situation with a little honest hedging. "Look, I'll do the best I can."

Her expression made it clear she didn't believe his best would be very good. She opened her mouth to speak, then as quickly clamped her jaws, evidently deciding voicing her opinion would be a waste of breath. With a sigh, she turned away and indicated an array of display windows. "This is Wittering Mercantile."

Mary had thought, when she dashed into town to do some shopping while Miz Witty read her book, she would be free of Bonn Wittering. His kiss had been a shock to her senses, too stimulating and extraordinary for her peace of mind, especially since she'd spent the past two years learning to loathe him.

How ironic that Fate had forced him directly into her path when she'd so badly needed distance, time to untangle her emotions. Even after he'd run into her, she'd desperately tried to get away, but he'd thrown in that monkey wrench about Miz Witty's birthday gift. If there was one person she couldn't deny, it was Miz Witty. Even if it required being in contact with this smooth, playboy grandson—and he *was* smooth.

She'd experienced the odd moments when she'd almost liked the guy. Well, not liked, exactly, but—well, yes, for scattered fractions of seconds she'd *liked* the guy. His eyes never failed to disarm her. She'd read somewhere that the eyes were the windows to the soul. Why then, when she looked into Bonn Wittering's eyes, where she *should* see self-serving, smarmy charm, was she always astonished to find what looked like deep sincerity and honest regret for the way he'd treated his grandmother? Or was the truth simply that she was too unworldly to recognize the snake in the man suit?

He held the door as she preceded him into Wittering Mercantile. Once inside the general store with its wooden display shelves and rough-hewn appeal, she automatically aimed toward what she'd planned to buy. Not until she was in the toy department, scanning the doll section, did she realize Bonn stood beside her. She glanced at him, confused. "I thought you were going to look at compact disc players."

He surveyed the array of brightly packaged dolls, then returned his attention to her. "I thought that was where we were going." He picked up a boxed doll, dressed like a movie star. Examining it, his expression grew as close to amused as she could recall seeing. "I'm just guessing, but I don't think this is a compact disc player."

Witnessing the near smile and the mirth in his eyes sent a wayward thrill skittering along her spine. She quickly pulled her gaze away. "My little sister's birthday is August third. She's dying to have a Hollywood Queenie doll."

He examined the platinum-haired toy swathed in a formal gown. "That's what this is?"

"She's the 'Senior Prom' Hollywood Queenie."

He chuckled. Though cynical, the sound was rich and charged with enough electricity to make the hair at her nape stand up. "She wasn't at my senior prom," he said.

Against her will she glanced at him, finding that statement hard to fathom. If anybody had the sexual magnetism to assure himself a date to his senior prom with the blondest, shapeliest girl in town, he did. "Why not?" She bit her tongue for asking. How dare she care!

He replaced the doll. "From age nine until eighteen, I went to an all-male boarding school. You do the math."

She found herself smiling, then quickly fixed her expression. "Right, I forgot. But—your school didn't have a senior dance—to celebrate graduating?"

"To celebrate graduating, my school handed out a packet with final grades, a diploma in Latin and a small, gray envelope for depositing our room keys. It was touching," he said, his tone sarcastic.

"Tear-jerking," she quipped back, turning away to inspect the Hollywood Queenie dolls on display. She didn't intend to exchange childhood memories with this man.

She picked up the 'Senior Prom' Hollywood Queenie and looked at the price tag. Thirty-five dollars. She sighed and returned it to the counter. The fanciest ones were way too expensive. Those she could afford wore scanty cotton shorts and tops. She would give anything to be able to buy Becca a really showy one—with a glittery gown, sparkling crown and all the accessories to satisfy a little girl's fondest fantasies. Becca had so little in her life that was cheery and fun. She picked up one with dark hair, clad in black, plastic slacks and a belly-baring knit top. Twelve dollars! She bit her lip, trying to decide if her budget would allow it.

"You have a little sister?"

She nodded but resisted the urge to look at him. "Becca's five." She picked up a doll in a simple cotton, flowered sundress. It cost three dollars less.

"Do your folks live in Wittering?"

"No—well…" She glanced his way. Why was he still here? It was hard enough to make a choice that fit her budget as well as her longing to make Becca's life brighter without him muddying up her mind. "Actually, my father died when I was fifteen. Mom remarried seven years ago, to a man named Joe Lukins."

She tried to sound conversational, but her intense dislike for Joe tended to reveal itself in the mention of his name. "Mom got sick a couple of years ago, and passed away right before Christmas that year." She swallowed around the lump of grief that formed whenever she thought about her mother, a good woman who'd never had much luck in life. "Becca's my half sister. She lives with her father in a trailer park, down a side rode at the other end of Wittering."

"That's too bad," he said.

She frowned, confused. Did he read minds? Had he detected how much she hated the fact that little Becca lived with Joe Lukins, a heavy drinker who had a new live-in girlfriend every week? She detested the fact that Becca was being brought up in such a—a shoddy, unwholesome atmosphere. "What's too bad?"

His gaze lingered on hers, his expression serious. "About losing your mother and dad."

"Oh—yes. But you know all about how that feels, yourself."

He pursed his lips, nodding. "Yeah."

She made a production of picking up two dolls, comparing them with such seriousness you'd think world peace depended on her choice. "Uh—look—why don't you find the compact disc players. I don't want to keep you."

He was silent for a moment, and she sensed he was absorbing her abrupt dismissal. "Sure. Why don't I?"

She didn't watch him go, but she could hear the retreating thud of his boots. Once he was gone, she exhaled to relieve pent-up tension. Emotionally spent, she sank to the scuffed oak planking. Huddled there, she clutched a Hollywood Queenie doll in each fist, staring blankly at the floor.

CHAPTER FIVE

TAGGART sat at the kitchen table, blessedly alone. Pauline was gone, having finished her day's work. Absently, he gnawed at a chicken leg. He'd already eaten dinner with Miz Witty, in her room, but his serving sizes had been as small as hers. He had a sneaking suspicion Pauline dished him up those dainty portions so he would have to seek out more food. And in doing so, run into her.

What Pauline didn't realize was that Taggart Lancaster wasn't a top-notch defense lawyer for nothing. He knew how devious minds worked, so he steered clear of the kitchen until the cook was gone. As he ate, his thoughts trailed back to this afternoon in the mercantile. Eventually, Mary had joined him in the electronics department to help pick out several "easy listening" and classical compact discs she thought Miz Witty would enjoy.

He'd pulled out his billfold. Remembering just in time not to use his credit card, he extracted several twenties and a couple of fifties. As he paid, Mary had made a strange remark. "Look at all that cash,'' she'd said, sounding disgusted. ''For a minute, I forgot who and what you are.''

She'd turned and stalked out without another word. The next time he saw her was at dinner when he'd joined her and Miz Witty in the master suite. He and Mary had smiled and chatted, even laughed together at a funny story Miz Witty told about her childhood. Her friendly manner completely masked her utter abhorrence of him. He was sure the charade was taking its toll on her. Not that it wasn't stressful for him, but for entirely different reasons.

He dropped the chicken bone to his plate and wiped his hands on the napkin in his lap. Brooding, he finished the mashed potatoes and broccoli, then lounged back in his chair, sipping his coffee. He had a headache. Possibly from the altitude. *Yeah, right, Lancaster,* he jeered silently. *It's the altitude. It has nothing to do with the stress of trying to kill an attraction to a woman who despises you to the depths of her soul.* Why was it so hard? It wasn't like she was coming on to him, using her wiles to subtly seduce him! She hated him for Pete's sake!

He knew, intellectually, that she didn't really hate *him,* just who she thought he was. ''It doesn't make any difference who she hates or thinks she hates,'' he mumbled. ''Falling in love is not on your agenda.''

His cell phone rang, jarring him from his thoughts. He shifted in his chair, drawing it from a back pocket. He glanced at the display and recognized the number. Lee. Grimacing, he set down his coffee mug. He hoped her call was business, but doubted it. "Lan—" He cut himself off, remembering he was not Taggart Lancaster while sitting in the kitchen where anybody passing by might hear. "Hi, Lee," he said, unable to disguise his morose frame of mind.

"Well, hi to you, too. You don't have to sound so excited," she said, sarcastically.

"Sorry, Lee. I'm just tired."

"You? Tired? I didn't think you knew the word." She laughed, a honeyed, purring sound. He rubbed his eyes. As he'd feared, this wasn't a business call. She didn't laugh like that in the office. "Have you been out mountain climbing all day?"

"That's what I'm doing now," he said, his tone dispassionate. "As a matter of fact, I'm hanging from a cliff by one hand."

She laughed again. "You're such an idiot, baby."

"No argument there," he said. "The reminder's superfluous." *Not only about the fact that I'm an idiot,* he thought, *but your use of "baby" leaves me no hope that you've reconciled yourself to the fact that we no longer have a relationship outside work.*

"So, how's the little game going?"

He dropped a forearm to the table and turned his mug in circles to help defuse his restlessness. "Let's just say, being the degenerate grandson of the beloved matriarch of a small town isn't everything it's cracked up to be."

"Poor Taggart," she murmured, her tone coyly sexual. "Maybe I should come out there and give you a back rub—or something."

He winced. Eyeing the ceiling he decided to change the subject fast. The last thing he needed right now was Lee's sexual innuendoes cloaked in chitchat. Glancing around to make sure nobody lurked in the doorway, he asked, "Say, Lee, what's happening with that Margolis case?"

She didn't sound happy about the abrupt switch in topics, but she was a good lawyer, so she familiarized him with the latest.

He absorbed the news. "Considering how bad it could have been, if we get off with a fine, I'll consider it a win."

He heard a sound and glanced toward it. Mary had walked in and was reaching for a mug. He watched her pour herself coffee as Lee returned to her back rub offer. He had no choice but to cut her off. "Look, I've got to go. I've—got company."

"Oh? Well—later then." Lee sounded reluctant to end the call. "Have a nice vacation, baby."

"Don't bet the farm." Before Lee could respond, he flipped the phone closed and replaced it in his hip pocket.

Mary turned away from the green tile counter, her mug of coffee clutched in both hands. Frowning, she settled her glance on him.

After several grim, still seconds, he nodded a solemn greeting. "Evening," he said, wondering why she hadn't sprinted out the door once she'd poured her coffee.

She eyed him with suspicion. "Who was that, your lawyer?"

"What?" Her question caught him off guard. He stalled, unsure what to say, since he didn't know how much she'd heard.

She sipped her coffee, maintaining eye contact over the rim of her mug. When she finally lowered the cup, she said, "You made a remark about only having to pay a fine being like a win."

He absorbed her statement. Considering who she thought he was, he supposed his end of the conversation could have sounded that way— Bonn's lawyer advising him on some legal transgression, and the near miraculous possibility that he might get off with only a monetary fine. "Oh—right. Yeah. That was my lawyer." It wasn't quite a lie. Lee was indeed a lawyer, who had been, and still wanted like hell to be, his very own—on the most intimate level.

"Doesn't your lawyer get tired of bailing you out of trouble?"

Admittedly weary of wrangling to keep his white collar clients—including Bonn—from paying too dearly for their crimes and misdemeanors, Taggart shrugged. "That's what lawyers are paid to do."

For the second time that day, she shook her head at him, the corners of her pretty mouth turning down in open disapproval.

What a shock.

She looked away for a moment, chewed her lower lip, then focused on him again. "As much as I dislike you, Mr. Wittering, I am even *more* revolted by lawyers who make their livings saving rats from sinking ships."

Her unwelcome frankness didn't do his ego any good. Up until now, she'd insulted the man she thought he was. Little did she know she was finally insulting the man who was actually in the same room with her.

He met her disparaging gaze with a poker face. "A million lawyer jokes prove you're not alone in your low opinion. Even so, defense attorneys are an integral part of our justice system." For some reason he had to know her particular reasons for hating attorneys. "What did a lawyer ever do to you?"

She blinked, seeming unsettled by the question. When she continued to stare wordlessly, he coaxed, "I might be a lot of bad things, but people tell me I'm a good listener."

She inhaled, as though for strength. "Not that I think you really care," she said, "...but I'll tell you, just so you'll know how regular people live—and get so-called justice. My dad was in a car accident. It wasn't his fault. He was badly hurt and didn't have enough insurance to cover the medical bills, so he was forced to sue. Dad's lawyer was a nice, average guy from a nice, average firm. The rich jerk who hit our car had lots of money and hired a high-priced firm to defend him. Daddy's lawyer could win in a good, honest fight. But he'd never gone up against a tableful of smooth-talking, amoral sharks."

She shook her head, looking sad. "It was a massacre. By rights, Mr. Moneybags should have paid my father's medical bills, plus punitive damages, but his lawyer got him off scot-free." Her voice quivered and she swallowed. "Dad never fully recovered. That slime trail of a law firm might as well have stabbed Daddy in the heart." She lay her mug on the countertop, her gaze shimmering, her features hard.

Taggart didn't know what to say. The legal system wasn't perfect. No legal system was without flaws. Of course, Mary would only see her father's side of things. He could have been more at fault than she wanted to believe, but bringing that up would serve no purpose. "I'm sorry about what happened to your dad," he said, meaning it. "What can I say?"

"Nothing. You can't help being born rich," she said. "But try getting justice without money sometime. See how it goes."

He didn't speak. Fighting the wayward urge to drag her in his arms, he took a sip of his coffee.

"So what trouble did you get into that your high-priced shyster's gotten you off with only a fine?"

High-priced shyster? That was painful, and not a pretty picture of his career choice. Yet, even as antagonistic as she was, this was the longest conversation they'd shared outside Miz Witty's presence. At least, the longest initiated by Mary. He couldn't imagine what had caused this sudden need of hers to break her vow to avoid him like the plague. Some kind of morbid curiosity about the black sheep mentality? "I thought you were the one who told me to stay out of your way." He sat back, eyeing her with curiosity. "What's with the examination? Do I dare hope you've decided to write my biography?"

She crossed her arms and pointedly looked away, seeming disconcerted, as though she wasn't sure herself why she was still there. "I have absolutely no interest in you, Mr. Wittering," she said, tentatively meeting his gaze again. "I just— well, Miz Witty is important to me, and I don't like to think you'll end up hurting her any more than you already have, that's all."

He experienced a knife twist in his gut. Wasn't he walking a tightrope, doing his damnedest not to? "What do you mean?" he asked.

"I mean..." She walked to the table, leaned forward, placing the flats of her hands on the polished pine surface. "I mean, I don't know what kind of trouble you've gotten yourself into, or what kind of trouble you're likely to get into after you leave." Her face was only a short distance away now, her smoky-brown eyes glistening with emotion. "If you go to *jail*, that would destroy her. She really is in fragile health—her heart's not strong. A blow like that and—and..."

Her voice broke. She swallowed hard and he could tell she was attempting not to cry. "I'm begging you, Bonn—be a greedy pig if you have to. Be a womanizing weasel if you must. I don't care. But *please* don't do anything to get yourself put in prison. It would kill her."

Her reproach grated on him, but he hid it. *Blast!* That's all he needed. More pressure. With

Bonn in serious trouble, charged with insider trading, getting him off without jail time would take
every ounce of Taggart's legal expertise, not to
mention a magic wand. ''She has a bad heart?''
he asked, unaware he'd even considered the question until he heard himself ask it.

''Of course. I told you that in my letters.''

Damn. He should have insisted Bonn let him
read those confounded letters to avoid this kind
of screwup. ''Right,'' he mumbled. Her plea
weighed down on him, a choking burden. He
couldn't look away from her eyes, couldn't miss
her suffering, glinting in the depths like shards of
glass, cutting him and making him bleed.

He laid a hand over hers and squeezed encouragingly. The idea of touching her that way hadn't
entered his mind, at least not on a conscious level.
He simply felt a need to comfort her, ease her
fear. ''Mary, I...'' He paused. What could he say?
That she affected him like no other woman since
Annalisa? Yeah, that would be bright. He could
just hear that speech.

*''Mary, you're driving me crazy. I don't love
you. I don't want to, but I can't get you out of
my head. I never hoped to find another woman I
could care for as deeply as I did for Annalisa. I
have my memories, and that's all I need. But ever
since I met you, I've felt like I'm on fire.*

*I've been lying to you since that first moment.
I'm not Bonn Wittering. I'm his lawyer—yes, a
high-priced, smooth-talking lawyer, the vermin
you hate even worse than you hate Bonn. And
even as sleazy a shyster as you think I am for
what I do, I might not be able to save Bonn from
prison. If I can't, I hope Miz Witty's heart can
stand the blow.*

*And last but far from least—if you can overlook
the little matter of finding me, and all I do, contemptible, could you please do me the kindness of
releasing me from whatever hold you have over
me before I go completely mad?''*

Yeah, Taggart. Excellent speech. He closed his
mouth, one of the few times in life he'd been at
a loss for words. The only emotions getting
through were the gnawing pain in his heart and
the torture of his struggling conscience. The nagging obligation to keep a friend's confidence, the
haunting knowledge that the truth about who he
was, and the trouble Bonn was in, if revealed,
could only cause heartache for innocents. And if
what Mary said about Miz Witty's heart was real,
the truth might even kill.

He scanned Mary's face, those soft, somber
eyes and sad, yet bewitching lips. Must every expression on her face, every movement she made,
bedevil him? He was astonished and troubled, at

the sense of oneness he felt merely holding her hand.

Her distraught gaze held his, questioning. Somehow she seemed less angry, less disapproving. "What—Bonn?" she asked in a hushed whisper. "What were you going to say?" Her face was so close he could feel the warmth of her breath. Her lips were mere inches from his, tantalizing cruelly.

What he'd started to say, *wanted* to say, was out of the question. He only knew he held her hand—a hand she hadn't yet withdrawn from his touch. He grasped at mental straws. What could he say? What would reassure her? He couldn't be positive Bonn wouldn't go to prison. He couldn't even be sure something wouldn't go wrong any moment, that he would be found out. If that happened, or if Bonn went to prison, he couldn't assure her Miz Witty's health wouldn't suffer.

She dropped her eyes before his steady gaze and seemed to focus on his hand, holding hers. "Why the long silence?" she whispered. "Why the hesitation?"

His gaze caressed her face, the dark hair spilling over her shoulders. He inhaled her scent, delicately erotic. She was so lovely, so loyal, so unhappy. He ached to fold her in his arms, tell her everything would be all right. But he was no miracle worker, no fortune-teller. He was only a man,

an imperfect creature who'd allowed himself to
be pulled into an impossible situation, out of obligation and loyalty.

His internal battle tore at his insides. What to
say? How much truth did he dare? How much lie
must he swear? At long last, and with difficulty,
he found his voice and his answer. "Mary," he
said gruffly, sincerely, "I can't make any promises to you."

She lifted her gaze to meet his, her eyes large
and luminous. Rather than looking forlorn and af-
flicted, as he'd thought she would, she appeared
mystified. "I'm surprised," she said.

"Surprised?"

"I'm surprised you didn't just promise." She
searched his face as though attempting to probe
his thoughts. "Why bother with honesty?"

He understood what she meant. Why hadn't he
put her at ease with a smooth lie? After all, the
unreliable Bonn she knew was renowned for taking the path of least resistance, tossing off empty
promises along the way without hesitation or regret.

Because I am not Bonn. We are two entirely
different people! Mary O'Mara, you are shrewder
than you know. Weary of the hoax, but knowing
he had no choice, he lifted his hand from hers and
sat back in his chair. "It must be the thin air,"
he improvised, feigning cynicism. "Don't worry,

Miss O'Mara. I'll be my slithery, old self in no time.''

She straightened abruptly. Lacing her fingers in a tight ball she regarded him with coldness. The sight of her renewed abhorrence filled him with a cruel and perverse sense of loss.

Raking his fingers through his hair, he gave himself a minute to clear his head of the effects of her nearness and her touch, and to deal with her renewed hostility. Excruciating tasks, especially after so recently seeing—*something* in her eyes. Something new and contrary to all reason.

Taggart lay in bed, wide awake, staring up at his ceiling. Sleep seemed to be a luxury of some dimly remembered past, considering how much of it he'd managed to get since his arrival in Wittering on Monday. Here it was Wednesday night at—he checked his watch—correction, two-thirty, Thursday morning. He could count on one hand the hours he'd actually *slept* in this bed.

His mind roamed to terrain he'd traveled too much in the past few hours—to earlier that evening. He recalled vividly the image of Mary leaning over the table, imploring him to consider Miz Witty's health as he went about his wicked lifestyle. *Be a greedy sleaze and a womanizer, but don't go to jail.*

"Be a greedy sleaze?" he murmured. "Be a greedy sleaze *and* a womanizer?" He didn't know what she meant. What did she think Bonn did? Cheat at cards? Bilk vulnerable heiresses out of their fortunes? He frowned. That couldn't be it. Bonn had his own money. He might be a skirt chaser, but he didn't lie to women. Didn't cheat them. While women were dating Bonn, they had a great run, plenty of luxury and fun. As a matter of fact, most of Bonn's ex-girlfriends remained his friends. He was that hard to dislike. He was generous, spontaneous, amusing, and he didn't have a mean bone in his body. He had a quick temper, true. And he was rash, but never mean.

And he didn't gamble. Not even for matchsticks. Sometimes he bet on football games if there was a pot going at the gym, but who didn't? For the life of him, Taggart couldn't imagine why Mary O'Mara would call Bonn a greedy sleaze.

He rubbed his eyes. What in blazes difference did it make what Mary O'Mara called him? "Get your mind off the woman," he grumbled. "She thinks Bonn is the devil incarnate and his lawyer is his evil twin. There's nothing you can do about it. So shut up and get some rest."

Since staring at the ceiling wasn't working, he rolled to his stomach and closed his eyes. "Closing your eyes is a start," he muttered. "Think of something boring."

Somewhere in his mental meandering, he heard a noise that didn't mesh with the usual Rocky Mountain night sounds he'd become accustomed to during long, sleepless nights. A tapping, rapid and incessant, intruded into his consciousness. He opened his eyes. What was that? It sounded like a woodpecker, pecking on his window.

He heard something else in addition to the tapping, like a voice. But he couldn't make out what it said. He came up on his elbows, shaking his head. Had he gone to sleep after all? This had to be a dream.

He heard the tapping again, then quite clearly he heard someone call out a name—Bonn. He shifted around and sat up, his attention instantly drawn to the side window of his bedroom. To his astonishment, he saw the silhouette of a head and shoulders outside the glass. *Good Lord,* his bedroom was on the second floor! Who could be outside his window? ''What the...'' He threw back the bedcovers and jumped up.

Hardly a babe in the woods where criminals were concerned, Taggart cautiously checked out the shadowy figure. It was clear, even from where he stood, the person outside wasn't a man. And making all that racket, if she were a burglar, she was never going to be a success.

He walked to the window and peered out. *Hell!* It was Pauline, the amorous cook! "What are you doing?" he asked, through the glass.

"Let me in, Bonn," she called in a loud whisper. "Hurry! I'm afraid this trellis won't hold much longer."

He had an urge to tell her she'd better scamper back down, then. Unfortunately, even though he'd known her for a very short time, he sensed she would rather perch out there until the thing collapsed and sent her plunging to her death rather than voluntarily climb down. Hating the need to, knowing no good could come of it, he unlocked the window and raised it. Before he could say anything, she pitched forward into his arms. Taken so by surprise, he nearly toppled backward but managed to retain his balance. "Whoa!" he said, as she grabbed him around the neck. "What do you think you're doing?"

She giggled, clinging. "Well, when the mountain won't go to the molehill..." she let the sentence die, as though it spoke for itself.

His temper frayed from stress and lack of sleep, Taggart's attempt to remain sympathetic to Pauline's underlying feelings of inferiority was evaporating fast. He reached up to detach her stranglehold. "Then the molehill climbs in Mohammed's bedroom window?"

"Who?"

"Never mind." What in blazes was he going to do about this woman? In the strict, all-male boarding school where he'd grown up, he'd been taught to treat women with the utmost respect, to ignore uncouth or vulgar behavior, respond as a gentleman, no matter what. He had a feeling the school's ultra-proper, puritanical faculty had not come up against anybody like Pauline Bordo. And when he said "against" he meant that *literally.*

She stretched on tiptoe and smooched his jaw. "I couldn't sleep. It killed me to think of you here—*all alone.* I had to sneak over and climb up, make sure you aren't lonely."

He grasped her wrists, compelling her to release him. "That's very—sociopathic of you."

"Yes, I'm—I'm very sociopathic conscious!" She looked as sincere and civic-minded as she could manage, considering she'd climbed in a near-stranger's bedroom window. "I rescued a cat from a tree, once. And every year at the Founder's Day celebration, I raise more money for charity than anybody else who volunteers for the kissing booth."

He released her wrists. Before she could re-grab his neck, he gripped her shoulders and pressed her an arm's length away. "I'm sure you're a credit to the community," he said as civilly as he could, under the circumstances. Now, the problem was, how to gently make her understand her playboy sex fantasy was not going to happen.

"Thank you." She smiled, reveling in his whispered compliment.

"You're welcome." Slipping a neighborly arm about her shoulders he aimed her toward the door. "I appreciate your dropping by, Pauline, but it's late, and—"

"Wait a second!" She slid out of his hold and faced him. Taggart hadn't had time to notice what she'd been wearing when she vaulted through his window, but with her escape she gave him no choice but to take note. Her legs braced wide, she stood before him in a light colored raincoat and jogging shoes. Her stance was the image of a superhero about to rip off her everywoman guise to reveal her secret, crime fighting identity.

Taggart's impression wasn't far off the mark. She yanked open her raincoat, flashing a skimpy, belly-baring T-shirt and tight shorts. He breathed a sigh of relief that she wasn't naked. He wouldn't have put it past her. "I thought we might—play," she said, her smile wily.

He didn't need this! He was dead on his feet. His eyes hurt with every blink, sandy from lack of sleep. Inhaling for patience, he tried hard to hold on to his attitude of weary tolerance.

He closed the coat and reached for the dangling sash. "Pauline, you're a beautiful woman. A fine person," he said, cinching the belt. "Not to mention, you're a fabulous cook. You're kind to animals and you volunteer for charity." Firmly but gently, he took her hand and tugged her toward the door. "I have the highest respect and admiration for you."

"You do?" she said, appearing a little shell-shocked. Clearly she hadn't expected to be marched from the bedroom she'd taken such a risk to get inside.

"Absolutely." Taggart got her headed down the stairs, still absorbed in his flattery. "I can't tell you when I've been more—impressed by a person's—diligence and, especially—her intrepidity."

"Intrepidity?" she asked, as they hit the bottom of the staircase. He glanced toward the front entrance and noticed the bright porch lights. Way too much visibility. With hardly a second's pause, he opted for the back door. The chances of anybody seeing Pauline leave the house via the rear entrance were almost nil. "Yes, intrepidity." He tugged her around the corner toward the kitchen. "I'm awed by yours."

He held her hand, coaxing her along. They entered the kitchen. It was so dark he couldn't see his hand in front of his face so he flipped on the overhead light. He hoped stark illumination would dampen Pauline's lurid inclination.

"What does intrepidity mean?" she asked.

"It means—courage, poise, self-reliance."

He had her almost to the back door when she dug in her heels, pulling to a halt. "Oh." She looked downcast. "I thought it meant—like—sexy."

Blast! He was so close to success he could almost taste it. "Well—Pauline, to be frank with you, I find courage, poise and self-reliance…" He tasted gall at the thought of finishing that sentence, but knew he had to forge on. One or two more compliments should get her out the door. "…very sexy."

She brightened. "No kidding?"

"No kidding." He encircled her shoulders with an arm, the better to guide her outside. But before he could get her through the door, she moved like lightning, slipping out of his grasp, unfastening her sash and shrugging out of her raincoat. She tossed it on the kitchen table. "Oh—that's just so—*sweet!*" She lunged, her arms going around his neck as she pressed herself provocatively against him. She smiled in invitation. "You look even better without clothes than I thought you would."

For the first time in his adult life, he wished he slept in a full set of pajamas instead of the black boxers he was wearing. "Look, Pauline—"

"Kiss me!" She puckered her lips.

He was losing patience fast. Her sexual pursuit was so aggressive it felt like hostility. What did he have to do to get rid of her, pick her up and toss her outside? It wasn't as though she didn't have a body most men would give their right arm simply to fondle. But, *dammit,* for all her voluptuous willingness, Pauline wasn't Mary O'Mara, and that was the bottom line. Taggart wanted Mary—in his heart, in his home, and in his bed.

He experienced a violent jolt, as though he'd been struck by lightning. *What had he been thinking?* He chewed on the thought and frowned. He *meant* Annalisa, not Mary O'Mara. He wanted Annalisa back. The pain of her loss whipped in quickly with a hammer-blow to the belly. He felt woozy and gut-punched, like a mugging victim. Shaking himself, he struggled back from the blow, locked his turmoil and pain away. He had to deal with his current problem.

The cook's inflexibility on the subject of having sex with Taggart was eroding his desire to remain civil. Dismayed at the prospect of beginning the "remove-Pauline-process" over again, he measured his words as carefully as he could. "I'm afraid you misunderstood what I meant when I said courage, poise and all that was— sexy."

She ran her tongue around her lips, an unsubtle come-on. "Enough talk," she said in a husky voice. "It's time for action."

He gritted his teeth and commanded himself not to fling little Miss It's-time-for-action over his shoulder and dump her in a heap onto the back lawn.

"My pretty, pretty man," she purred, brushing his lips with hers. "Oh, yummy."

Oh hell! He'd had it! He was no longer interested in getting Pauline out the door on her own power. She still clutched him about the neck. Without bothering to disengage her, or give her any other hints that she was mere seconds away from a brisk departure, he swooped down to grasp her behind the knees and lifted her in his arms.

Pauline giggled with glee. "Oh—you're so masterful!"

She had no idea he'd picked her up because it was the most expedient method of getting her out of the house. Good. In her deluded frame of mind, he could eject her more easily.

When he reached the kitchen table, bent on scooping up her overcoat, a wave of foreboding passed over him. He stilled. Though he'd heard no sound, detected no movement, a troubled, sideways squint told him what he suspected was true.

Mary O'Mara stood frozen in the kitchen doorway.

CHAPTER SIX

MARY stared in shocked disbelief at the lewd spectacle unfolding in the kitchen. She was well aware of Bonn's bad-boy reputation, but to witness him about to amuse himself with such—such depravity, right out in the open, was almost too obscene to comprehend—even seeing it with her own eyes.

Seeming to sense her presence, Bonn peered her way. Had she gasped? Screamed? She didn't think so, but somehow he'd realized she was there. An instant later, he plucked Pauline's coat from the table and carried her out the back door. Mary's last sight of the pair was Pauline hugging his neck, giggling wickedly. She closed her eyes but the vision remained, burned into her mind.

She didn't know how much time passed before he re-entered. It could have been a few seconds or a week. Her brain had gone numb. The fact that she was rooted in the kitchen doorway when he came inside, was another indicator that her brain had completely stopped functioning. The last thing she wanted was to be on hand to revisit the—the *incident* with him.

As he came inside and shut the door, his gaze met hers. He wasn't smiling, wasn't frowning. His expression was impassive, as though he'd just been outside getting a breath of air. Without speaking, he moved to the kitchen table and re-adjusted a chair that had been pushed slightly ajar. He turned around, faced her, grasping the top rung of the chair behind him with both hands. He pursed his lips and dipped his head in a brief nod. ''Evening.''

Was that all he intended to say? Did he have the audacity to act as though she had interrupted nothing out of the ordinary? As if stumbling upon a wild sex-capades in the kitchen was nothing to comment on?

Well, she didn't intend to pretend she didn't see what she saw! He could be blasé about his behavior, but that didn't mean she had to be! Her anger helped her brain reconnect with the rest of her body and she stomped into the kitchen, her bedroom slippers making slapping sounds as she moved past him to the stove.

She bent and clanged around in a cookware drawer beneath the oven until she found a small saucepan. She stood and slammed it down on a burner, tramped to the refrigerator, took out a milk carton, retraced her steps to the stove and sloshed milk into the pan. She could feel his eyes on her, but refused to acknowledge him. After replacing the carton in the refrigerator, she slammed the door so forcefully she could hear clinking and rattling inside.

"What are you doing?" he asked quietly.

From where she stood she could keep her back to him, so she did. "I'm having wild sex on the kitchen table, what does it look like?" She bit down hard on her lower lip. Why had she blurted that? Apparently, she'd felt an uncontrollable urge to needle him. Sarcasm was a well-accepted form of payback. However, bringing up sex for any reason was more like bashing herself in the head with a baseball bat than the pithy comeback she'd meant it to be. She squeezed her eyes shut and prayed for the power to disappear.

"I wasn't going to have sex on the kitchen table," he said, his tone composed.

She kept her eyes closed. *Drat!* Why had she opened up the very door she'd wanted so badly to nail shut? Mentioning the—the incident— hadn't been in her head at all! She'd planned to say she was playing the piano. What happened to, *"I'm playing the piano"?* Opening her eyes, she stared into the pan of milk and muttered, "I don't care whether you were or not."

"You might want to turn on the flame," he said. "Unless you like drinking cold milk out of saucepans."

She flinched. Where was her mind? She switched on the heat but refused to comment.

"We both had clothes on."

She was painfully aware of how much—rather how *little*—they where wearing. She refused to speak for fear her voice would break. How dare she feel jealous! Bonn Wittering was not worthy of any woman's honest affections.

"Pauline climbed in my bedroom window," he said. "When you came in, I was getting rid of her."

Blinking back idiotic tears, Mary pulled her terry robe closer about her and cinched up the sash. "I *really* don't care."

I really don't! I really don't! I really don't! she told herself, the screams of her denial deafening in her head. She would stamp out her wayward attraction for this amoral playboy or die trying! She bit her lip worriedly. *No! No! No negatives.* She would stamp out her attraction to him, no "ifs," "ands," or "buts," and positively no "or-die-tryings"!

"Pauline doesn't take no for an answer," he said.

Mary swallowed to dislodge the lump stuck in her throat. She struggled against her wayward feelings of envy for Pauline—of all people! "You two make a wonderful couple," she said, sounding hoarse. "You don't *give* no for an answer!"

The silence between them became drawn out and very dead.

At long last, he asked, "Did you see any actual sex going on?" Though his question was spoken quietly, in the bleak stillness it rang like steel striking against steel.

She jumped, her gaze bounding from steaming milk to the sea-green wall over the stove. Pressing a calming hand on her heart, she unwillingly revisited the scene in her mind. "Don't give yourself a halo just because I broke in on the foreplay."

"Foreplay?" His chuckle was deep and cynical and went through her like an electrical current. "Foreplay for that woman was the fifteen minutes she spent bursting through puberty."

Mary turned off the fire and carried the pan of steaming milk to the counter where the mugs were stored. She took one down from the shelf and poured herself some hot milk.

"Any left?" he asked.

She stared bleakly into the pan, still half full. She'd been in too much of a state of insane, envious hostility to care about waste when she'd filled the pan. She nodded.

"Would you mind pouring me some?"

Without comment she grabbed another mug from the shelf above the coffeemaker and emptied the rest of the milk into it. She carried the pot to the sink and ran water into it, then retrieved the drinks. On feet of lead, she moved to the table. "Here." She shoved a mug at him.

Pulling out a chair she sat down and set her steaming milk on the pine surface. An instant later, in a horrible flash, she remembered what had almost gone on there. *"Ewe!"* She vaulted up and shoved the chair back. It scraped loudly against the pine floor as it skidded away. "Yuck!" She spun to face the sink. "I don't think I'll ever be able to eat food there again."

"Come now." He sounded weary. "It's just a table that had a raincoat, and nothing else, on it."

Wood scraping against wood told her he was seating himself. She shifted to peer at him as he took a sip of hot milk. He looked tired around the eyes. Even fatigued, he still had a mesmerizing gaze. A swath of wavy, ebony hair fell across his forehead, creased in what appeared to be weariness or adversity, or both. Otherwise, he looked as yummy as Pauline had cooed.

He rested his forearms on the table. Wide shoulders drew Mary's gaze, even slouched as he was. His broad, contoured chest rose and fell as he breathed. He certainly had the physique of a playboy, at least what she presumed a playboy's chest must be like. To attract women a playboy's body would need to be superior to other men's. It must be the kind of body that could seduce women the way firelight seduced a moth—so attractive, so innately seductive, the moth, and the woman, would ignore inherent dangers.

His steaming mug sat between his hands. In the silence, he clenched and unclenched his fists. His gaze remained focused on the hot milk but he seemed to be looking inward, pondering some dark, difficult thought.

Even as grim and exhausted as he looked, he was a compelling presence. So much so, Mary found herself pulling up her chair and taking her seat—like that moth fluttering dangerously near the flame. The man had magical powers. That was the only way she could explain the fact that she had seated herself kitty-corner to him at the table where he and Pauline had, moments ago, almost...

She pushed the thought back into a deep, dark corner of her mind and sipped her milk. Unable to help herself, she silently observed him. Her emotions were a hodgepodge of dire suspicion and palpitating curiosity. From his fixed expression, she could tell he'd gone so far away in his head, she didn't think he knew she was in the room. Yet, he had the capacity to draw her, even detached from the here-and-now, as he was.

His nearness both disturbed and excited her with excitement winning out by a hair. What happened to the levelheaded Mary, the objective,

hardworking caregiver, who knew the difference
between right and wrong, fair and unfair, worthy
and unworthy?

What happened to the Mary who knew for a
fact that Bonn Wittering was a self-serving reptile? She'd come to know this as an absolute, un-
debatable truth through their many, fruitless cor-
respondences. Until she'd made up that lie about
Miz Witty considering dropping him from her
will, all she'd gotten for her begging and pleading
that he visit were half-baked promises he never
kept and slick excuses explaining away his negligence.

So why, when she looked into his eyes, could
she see nothing of the man she'd come to know?
Why did she think she could detect in those
earthy depths, subtle hints of wisdom, vague
whispers of nobility in his character?

Even now, with the spectacle of him entwined
with Pauline wrecking havoc in her mind, why
could she see nothing villainous or cowardly in
his eyes? She scanned his face, puzzled. His features were forbidding, his firm, sensual lips set in
a grim line. His tensed jaw, darkened by the
shadow of a beard, gave him a stirring aura.

While he looked inside himself, unaware she
was even there, Mary searched his eyes. Where
was the lecher? Where did the snake lurk—the
self-centered bum who'd made this trip to sweet

talk his grandmother so she wouldn't cut him out of her will? Mary knew all his tricks, his evasions, knew his black character as well as she knew her own name.

Yet as hard as she probed, she could only see a weary, contemplative man—a man very conflicted about something. She'd never thought of Bonn as a person to reflect on anything longer than it took to decide on the next thrill, and certainly not one to fritter away a moment in serious thought, especially if the thought were troublesome or gloomy.

Finishing her milk, she thudded her mug to the table. Just because the man had eyes that could hide his shifty character was no reason to be taken in by him! *She knew him!* This pensive musing over Bonn Wittering was almost as crazy as her senseless attraction to him. What was she doing wasting her time conjuring up some deep, emotional goings-on in his head? Most likely, he was only brooding because she'd interrupted his sexual hijinks, leaving him frustrated and ungratified.

Annoyed with herself for having soft and gooey thoughts about a man she knew all too well, she nudged his arm. "Hey, wake up."

He blinked, coming out of his trance. Shifting his gaze her way, he met her frown straight-on. "What?"

"Drink up. No use crying over spilt sex."

His brow crinkled further, as though what she said made no sense to him.

"Drink the milk." She indicated his mug. "It'll help you sleep."

Creases of affliction between his eyes deepened as his glance drifted over the mug, then back to her. "I don't believe in sleep." He dragged a hand through his hair. "It's highly overrated."

"Then why ask for the milk?" She wondered why she was still there. Her milk was gone. She needed to get to bed so the beverage could weave its sedating spell. She was afraid, after witnessing barely-clothed-Bonn-with-the-sexy-chest-and-stunning-eyes, any tranquilizing gift the milk contained would have its work cut out for it.

"Why did I ask for the milk?" He repeated her question in a whisper, as though pondering it. He shifted his focus to the mug, then slowly shook his head. "I guess…" Unreadable, hooded eyes sought hers. His nostrils flared as though tormented about something. "…I don't know why," he said woodenly. She sensed he was lying, but couldn't tell if he was lying to her or to himself. She rubbed her temples at the crazy thought.

Placing the flats of his hands on the table, he pushed up. "Good night, Miss O'Mara," he said through clenched jaws. Before he walked away, his gaze held hers, in a split second filling her mind with the unforgettable image of a man and his iron-bound firmness of purpose—a man in pain, torn apart by private demons.

A full minute after he'd left the kitchen, she still couldn't catch her breath.

Miz Witty's birthday party was in full swing, the house packed to the rafters with laughing, chatting guests. Mary's most vivid memory of the party so far was of Bonn, as he'd gallantly carried his grandmother down the stairs and swept her into the living room. The two of them had made quite a spectacular entrance. Miz Witty in a long, royal blue velvet dressing gown and Bonn in navy slacks and a matching mock turtleneck that showed off bulging muscle as he whisked his beaming grandmother into a roomful of applauding friends.

Mary squeezed her eyes shut, forcing the memory from her head. Getting her mind on business she checked her watch. Nine o'clock. She glanced around the living room, filled with casually dressed partygoers. Furniture had either been removed temporarily to the basement or pushed to the walls, the Persian rug taken away, to create space for dancing on the polished oaken planks.

Miz Witty sat in her wheelchair among a group of well-wishers, having a gay old time. Her delighted tittering could be heard above conversation and dance music that filled the air.

Gifts had been opened, the wrapping paper and ribbon debris cleared away. The festivities had settled into a comfortable gathering of old friends, grazing the refreshments on the dining room table or just sitting and talking. A few of the younger couples danced. Bonn's compact disc player had been a big hit. Music wafted over the buzz of chitchat.

Mary scanned the dancers. Several couples swayed to the sultry melody, including Bonn and a giggly teenager. Miz Witty's grandson had spent a great deal of time on the dance floor. Mary had to admit that most of his dancing was the result of invitations by goofy-grinning Wittering women, ranging in age eighteen to eighty. They all seemed to find their most infamous native son's charm impossible to resist. From Mary's vantage point, the black sheep of Wittering had treated each dance partner with the gallantry of a truly accomplished charmer.

The lights were low, the mood cheerful, even romantic, if one's mood could be coerced in that direction. Mary, unfortunately, was in no mood for either romance or cheer. Besides the difficult problem of having to appear delighted to be around Bonn in Miz Witty's presence, she'd had a bad blow of a personal nature. Joe Lukins had promised faithfully to allow Mary's half sister, Becca, to attend the party.

Becca loved Miz Witty like family, and the little girl had been promised an overnight stay. Little Becca would have loved being at the birthday party—with the cake and ice cream and noisemakers. She would have loved a visit with Miz Witty, and her doting big sister. However, typical of Joe, he'd called at the last minute saying Becca had a cold. Preposterous! He was simply too contemptible to care that he was breaking his little girl's heart.

Mary had pleaded to be allowed to come pick up Becca as they'd arranged, since Joe's drunk driving record had caused his license to be revoked. But Joe insisted his daughter was not physically up to a party. When Mary demanded she be allowed to come take a look at the girl, Joe told her he was Becca's father and his word was law. He warned her if she came over she'd be wasting her time, because he wouldn't let her inside his trailer.

Angry, frustrated and hurting for her little sister, Mary escaped into the kitchen only to find herself alone with Pauline. That was just peachy! All she needed was for the cook to start in on a blow-by-blow description of her kitchen romp with Bonn. Well, she'd have to chance it. She was too unhappy to fake a party smile for one more second, and she didn't have to fake one in front of Pauline.

The cook sat at the kitchen table, staring blankly at a piece of half-eaten birthday cake. She glanced up when Mary came in, but didn't speak, didn't smile. She looked strangely depressed, which wasn't like Pauline.

The kitchen air smelled luscious with the lingering scents of baking cake and the varied, delectable snacks the cook had whipped up for the party. One thing she had to give Pauline credit for, she was as passionate about her cooking as she was about her sex life. For the millionth time, she shoved back the memory of last night and headed to the stove. She hefted the teakettle to check how much water was in it. It felt full so she turned on the heat. When she was dejected over some mean stunt Joe Lukins pulled to keep Becca away from her, a cup of chamomile tea helped blunt her bloodthirsty urges.

"How's the party going?" Pauline asked, sounding depressed.

Mary turned away from the stove and looked at her, so uncharacteristically blue. Working to get her mind off her own troubles, Mary walked to the table and pulled out a chair. "The party's going great. The cake and all the hors d'oeuvres are wonderful. You outdid yourself." She indicated Pauline's half-consumed piece of birthday cake. "Aren't you feeling well? It's the best carrot cake I've ever eaten, so it can't be that you don't like it.''

Pauline hunched there, elbows on the table, her hands pressed to the sides of her face as though they were holding up her head. "I'm not hungry.''

Mary crossed her forearms on the table, peering at the cook. "You usually love parties, especially if there's dancing.'' She indicated the closed kitchen door. "Go on out, have some fun. I can hold down the kitchen for a while.''

Pauline shifted her morose gaze to Mary and made a face. "I just couldn't. Besides the last batch of cheezy pizza puffs is in the oven.''

Mary didn't want to pry, but this sad woman who couldn't eat her own delicious cake, and— Mary noticed belatedly—whose flannel shirt was buttoned all the way to her neck, was not the Pauline she'd seen cavorting in this very kitchen in the wee hours of the night. "What's wrong?'' she asked. "It's not like you to be depressed.''

Pauline heaved a big sigh. "I know.'' She indicated the kitchen door, presumably referring to the party going on not far away. "It's because of Bonn.''

Mary experienced a sharp pang in her heart. Maybe she didn't want to hear this after all. "Oh—uh—well, if it's private...''

Pauline sagged back in her chair, allowing her arms to dangle. "Oh, well, you saw us—in here. You know what happened." She lolled her head back to stare at the ceiling. "You saw me making a big, dorky fool of myself."

Mary was startled by the declaration. "That's not true, Pauline," she said, feeling compassion for the busty bombshell and unsure why. "I didn't see him fighting you off."

Pauline reclined her head to the side so she could meet Mary's gaze. She chewed on her lower lip for a moment before she answered. "Oh, he did fight me off. He was nice about it, but..." She shrugged. "When he got me bundled outside, he said as gentlemanly as you please, that I was a desirable woman, but he—he *cared* about somebody else, so he couldn't..." She shook her head, lifting her gaze to the ceiling. "I knew it was a brush-off. Who ever heard of a playboy turning down..." She paused, then clamped her mouth and her eyes shut.

Mary searched around in her head for something encouraging to say. Before she could come up with anything Pauline opened her eyes. "*Shoot,* Mary!" she said, her lower lip trembling. "Am I that unsexy that even a man who's a *well-known* sex machine has to lie, make up some lame story about being committed to some woman, just to get out of having sex with *me?*"

Mary was still having trouble absorbing Pauline's revelation about Bonn's rejection. She would never have thought of the man even considering a monogamous relationship. She didn't know what to say to help lift the cook out of her depression. She vividly remembered when Bonn kissed her. Of course, it hadn't meant a thing to him. No doubt he'd been slumming—the wealthy womanizer grabbing a taste of the hired help.

The idea unsettled her, tormented her—not just the reminder of Bonn's kiss, a sensual experience like no other she'd ever had—but of the vast difference in their stations. Though he'd blown his fortune, Bonn Wittering was born into privilege and luxury, received an expensive European education, traveled the world, made love to princesses, movie actresses and fashion models. Mary O'Mara, on the other hand, was born and raised in Wittering's rundown Trailer Town. She'd grown up wearing thrift shop castoffs, had only traveled as far away as Denver.

Whether Bonn truly had a significant other in his life or not, he hadn't found kissing her a breach of his moral code. Oh, he'd apologized, probably belatedly remembering his fidelity to the lady in question *didn't* include kissing the hired help, no matter how meaningless the act might be.

Pauline hunched forward, letting out a groan. She picked up her fork and began smashing bits of the cake. Feeling for the cook, Mary touched her arm. "Pauline, you're a wonderful woman. You're passionate, generous and open, and you're the best cook in this town." She squeezed her arm reassuringly. "I'm sure Mr. Wittering was being honest with you. He may be a notorious playboy, but he's still a human being, and human beings can fall in love."

Pauline glanced her way, her eyes shimmery, her expression full of suffering, so Mary went on, grasping at any straw. "He may not be able to feel the deep, forever kind of love that most of us feel, but it's reassuring to know he can be—faithful." *That* word, referring to Bonn Wittering, was difficult to get out, but for Pauline's tattered pride, she managed. "Now, go fix that face. I'll watch the pizza puffs. Don't let last night spoil your fun. Trust me, the man's not worth it. Get out there and dance, let him see you're fine. If you give his ego anything else to feed on he'll be too huge to walk through doors!"

Pauline blinked, a wan smile curving her lips. "You think so?" she asked, sounding like a little kid.

"I know so." Mary wasn't nearly as convinced as she pretended, but allowing Pauline to sit there stewing over a bum like Bonn Wittering would be a crime.

The teakettle began to whistle, so she stood. With a hand on Pauline's arm, she coaxed her to get up. "Go on. A little powder on that nose and you'll be as good as new."

Pauline obeyed, pushing up and swiping at a tear. "You're right. So what if he was lying."

"But I bet he wasn't," Mary insisted, trying to sound as though she believed it. Maybe the man was trying to be faithful. It wasn't probable, but it *was* possible. The teakettle shrieked, forcing her to break eye contact and hurry to remove it from the heat. After she got rid of the high pitched wail, she turned to face Pauline again. "I bet he was being honorable," she said. Maybe repeating it would make it more believable in time. "Some poor woman back in Boston has stolen his fickle little heart for a month or two. It could happen."

She walked to Pauline and grasped her by the upper arms, squeezing in an attempt to bolster her spirits. She had a sudden thought. "You know, Jed Swenson is out there. Do you think he keeps coming into the kitchen for glasses of water because he likes water that much?" Pauline did have admirers in town. Reminding her of that couldn't hurt.

The cook smoothed her hair back. "Jed is kinda sweet on me." She sniffed, straightened her shoulders. "Well—I guess I could go dance."

"You go. I'll handle the pizza puffs."

"Thanks, kid," she said, offering her first real smile. Mary felt better, too, and smiled back. Pauline's attitude changed. Mary could tell. She looked more determined than hurt, now. With a quick intake of breath and a resolute nod, Pauline grabbed her purse and repaired her makeup. A moment later, her features composed, she marched through the butler's pantry into the dining room.

The oven timer went off, so Mary took out the pizza puffs, deposited them on a waiting tray and added them to the goodies in the dining room. Her fake party smile was painful, even for the short time it took her to rid herself of the snacks and rush back into the safe haven of the empty kitchen.

She fixed herself a cup of chamomile tea and dropped into her chair at the kitchen table. She listlessly sipped the stuff, all too soon aware she was asking the same sort of soothing miracle from the tea she'd asked of last night's hot milk, which had failed her completely. She hadn't slept at all. And the tea, well, as she took the last sip, she felt the same degree of anger and frustration over Joe

Lukins' cruel manipulations of Becca as she'd felt while on the phone with him.

She heard the kitchen door open and glanced up, unsettled to see Bonn standing there. He wasn't smiling. Interesting how he could fake that party animal act hour upon hour, but the instant he was no longer required to play the part of charming houseguest, he dropped the mask like it burned his face. She was acting the same way, of course. They were both playing the same game, but for very different reasons.

She swallowed, nodded, trying to appear unruffled. "Yes?"

Holding the door just wide enough for her to see the glorious masculine package he was, he lounged against the wooden frame. "Someone named Sam said this was his dance. He asked if I'd locate you."

"What's the matter with Sam's powers of detection?"

Bonn lifted an eyebrow. "Would you like me to ask him?"

Mary sighed, shook her head. It was time to get over Joe Lukins and his heartlessness and get back to the party. After all, as Miz Witty's employee, she was a hostess of sorts. Hopefully dancing with Sam would help ease her anxiety. "I'll be right in."

He pursed his lips, nodded and turned away. The door silently closed behind him. Feeling strangely light-headed, she pressed her palms to the table, leaning heavily on them. How could she allow him to affect her that thoroughly with only a look? She'd seen no emotion in his eyes stronger than indifference, yet here she sat, too weak to stand! She sucked in a quivery breath, knowing she had no choice but to go back to the party.

Fine! Perfect! Once she rejoined the merry-making, she would be in the same room with Bonn. The only way dancing with Sam would be of any emotional aid to her would be if Miz Witty's troubling grandson disappeared. She held out little hope for that to happen, since he'd come to Wittering specifically to be with his grand-mother on her seventy-fifth birthday.

After a few more deep breaths, Mary was able to get up. She decided to enter the party via the butler's pantry that led into the dining room. She skirted the table, crowded with guests heaping their plates with delicacies. On her way across the foyer, she noticed Pauline and Jed sitting about halfway up the stairs. Their faces close, they smiled and whispered, oblivious to the party going on around them.

Mary had always liked Jed. A fellow Trailer Town kid, he was a shy, hardworking garage mechanic and a sweet guy. The tall, rawboned red-head had an obvious crush on the cook. As Mary passed them, Pauline giggled and patted his knee. Mary had a feeling Jed was going to have a very agreeable time tonight.

She entered the living room and headed toward the library in back. The two spaces were connected by double doors, swung wide. She didn't immediately see Bonn. That was a relief. Sadly, her relief was short-lived. Upon entering the library, she almost ran into him as he danced by with one of the town's matrons. The older woman chatted away and Bonn smiled at her, looking attentive and too gorgeous for Mary's peace of mind. She wondered if he was even listening to the woman, then pinched herself for caring.

She checked on Miz Witty, managed to refill her glass with cherry limeade punch before Sam spied her and pulled her onto the dance floor. Sam was a nice looking, compact man with a short, well-groomed beard and smiling blue eyes. She liked him, and she could tell he liked her. But she didn't feel the romantic pull of attraction she knew Sam wanted her to feel. And that was a shame. He owned Wittering's art gallery, and was quite a talented wood-carver himself. He'd been married and divorced, had a couple of kids living in California. He wanted to get married again, and he would have been good husband material for a country girl with no particular aspirations to live anywhere but these beautiful Rocky Mountains.

As he whirled her in his arms, she tried to be fascinated by his conversation. Too bad her mind seemed insistent upon recording where the dratted, unworthy Bonn Wittering was dancing.

The music changed, but Sam didn't let her go. As the instrumental melody began, a tittering and applause rose around them, and Mary realized Bonn had lifted Miz Witty from her wheelchair and was sweeping her around the dance floor in his arms.

The elderly Mrs. Wittering clung to Bonn's neck, laughing gaily as he waltzed her in a wide swathe around the room. The other couples, including Sam and Mary, stepped aside, allowing the birthday girl and her grandson the use of the floor. Mary held Sam's arm in a gesture of possessiveness she didn't feel. But he was her dance partner, and though they were sidelined, she still acted as though they were partners.

Maybe holding on to Sam was some unconscious mental aberration, wanting Bonn to know she, too, had admirers. Or possibly she just wanted Sam to feel this counted as ''a dance'' so she wouldn't have to spend a great deal of the evening with him. That thought made her feel guilty. She liked Sam, she really did. So why did she watch Bonn with such deplorable, ridiculous longing? Why did she tingle at the sight of his masculine grace as he danced? Why did she wish he held *her,* not her employer, in his strong, capable arms?

His smile was dashing, disarming. Though she knew it was a fraud, it still titillated, still thrilled her and made her knees weak. Maybe that was another reason she clung to Sam's arm, simply to remain upright.

The dance ended with a burst of applause, and Bonn returned his grandmother to her wheelchair. Miz Witty looked flushed, but otherwise perfectly fine. Even so, Mary decided she'd better check on her. She excused herself from Sam and walked to her employer. Unfortunately, Bonn remained beside his grandmother, who made his departure difficult by holding his hand with both of hers.

"Oh, Mary, dear," she said, smiling. "I've just told Bonny that I insist the two of you dance together." She beamed at her grandson as Mary disengaged one of Miz Witty's hands from Bonn's in order to check her pulse. It was rapid, but what sane woman's wouldn't be after being held in those manly arms and against such a magnificent chest?

She bit the inside of her cheek, punishing herself for having such a heated thought about Bonn. He might have fooled the rest of Wittering's female population with his smarmy appeal, but not

Mary O'Mara! ''He's quite a wonderful dancer,''
Miz Witty went on. She laughed, sounding like a
young girl. ''Of course, I'm so light on my feet,
I make anyone look good.''

Mary released her boss's hand and smiled at
her joke, though underneath she reeled with misgivings. Dance with Bonn? The idea had never
occurred to her—well, not in the past twenty-five
seconds. She cast him a furtive glance. He held
to his smile as their gazes met, but his eyes were
dark, unfathomable. She couldn't tell if he ab-
horred the idea of dancing with her or if it merely
bored him.

''Why, of course, Miz Witty,'' she said.
Pointing in the general direction of where she'd
left Sam, she improvised, ''I've promised the next
one—or two. Later, for sure.'' She glanced at
Bonn again but avoided meeting his eyes.
''Okay?''

He nodded, his grin cruelly stirring. ''I'll look
forward to it.''

The town's real estate agent, Maxie Unkle,
grabbed Bonn's free hand. ''My turn for a spin
around the floor.'' At five-eleven in her stocking
feet, Maxie towered over a lot of men. But not
Bonn. She pulled him onto the dance floor and
Mary forced her gaze not to follow. Excusing herself, she walked back to Sam, wishing she were
happier about it. He grinned at her, holding out

his arms. "Do I get this next dance, too?" he asked brightly.

She nodded, making herself smile. "If you'd like," she said, vowing to ignore Bonn with all her strength.

Sam took her into his arms and danced her around the room. Somewhere in the middle of the love song, Mary weakened and searched out the playboy. Their gazes met, clashing for several tense heartbeats before she was able to break eye contact. She wondered if he was thinking the same thing as she—if they weren't very careful, they might have to dance together.

She wished her foolish heart didn't leap at the very thought.

CHAPTER SEVEN

MARY descended the stairs after checking on Miz Witty, who was sleeping soundly, her birthday party long over. Pauline, Ruby the housekeeper, and Jed cleaned up the kitchen while Mary helped Miz Witty get ready for bed. Dead tired, they all decided tomorrow would be soon enough to re-arrange the furniture.

Jed and Pauline left around one-thirty. Moments later, Ruby trudged upstairs to her attic room. Mary envied the housekeeper, on her way to bed confident she would sleep soundly. Mary would give anything to be able to sleep! Yawning, she switched off the front porch light, walked outside and dropped into one of the cushioned metal chairs. From the elevated porch, she could see specks of illumination through the trees, street lamps and the occasional house light. Headlights flashed briefly beyond the trees, as cars traversed the town's byways—vacationers passing through, or rattletraps of local teens, out of school for the summer, cruising between houses of friends.

Even in Wittering humanity hummed along, twenty-four hours a day, just like the big cities. Mary rested her head against the cushioned chair-back, wishing she wasn't humming along twenty-four hours a day. She needed rest. Sleep. She yawned again, exhausted, but her brain was on fire. ''You can't sleep when your brain is smoldering,'' she muttered.

She massaged the bridge of her nose, angry with herself for feeling the same giddy desire for Bonn so many of Wittering's women exhibited at the party. She sighed long and low, making herself think of something else. *Anything* to put out the flames in her mind.

She stared up at the sky visible beyond the porch's roof. Stars twinkled there, looking clean and pure. It was hard to think of mean people, like Joe Lukins, or scheming playboys, like Bonn Wittering, under a sky full of sparkling stars.

As a little girl in the trailer park, she'd often escaped outside on summer nights like this. After her mom and dad were asleep, she'd taken the blanket off her bed, pulled herself out the trailer's window and clambered onto the roof. She would lay there for hours staring at the sky, wishing for a life as clean and bright as those stars. Somewhere outside the muddy, dreary Trailer Town.

Being a Trailer Town kid left its mark on Mary, making her a very determined person. Neither her mom nor dad finished high school, so Mary had studied hard. There'd been no money for college, and though she'd been eligible for scholarships, her dad's death along with the added burden of his unpaid medical bills, meant Mary was needed at home, to work, to help supplement her mother's waitress salary.

Even so, on one of those nights she'd lain awake on top of that trailer, she'd made a vow. College or no college, she would make something of her life. She had decided to become a nurse. She wanted to make a difference, and nurses made a difference. They could wear pure, white uniforms, and they got respect, something Trailer Town kids saw little of. Mary knew someday she would be a nurse, and she would get the respect she craved. That was half of her dream for a perfect life. The other half was to get Becca out of Trailer Town, out of Joe Lukins' mean-spirited custody.

To be a nurse and to have Becca to care for and love, that's all Mary wanted in the world. She knew if she worked hard, saved her money, she could eventually become a nurse. When Miz Witty had hired her and learned of her dream, she'd made Mary a promise. She'd told her she could always live in the beautiful Wittering home.

Since both of them were practically alone in the world, together, they had someone who felt a little like a family.

Miz Witty had even allowed Mary to redecorate the old nursery as a room for Becca, when she visited. It was a tiny room, directly across from the one Bonn occupied. Mary had painted it pink, perfect for a little girl. Such a living situation would be ideal for Becca, to live in a beautiful, clean, loving environment—except Joe Lukins would never agree.

Sadly, American courts didn't take custody away from a birth parent without very good reasons. Joe might not be an ideal father by any stretch of the imagination, but lots of children had it worse than Becca, and they weren't removed from their homes. It would take a miracle to get her half sister away from Joe. Mary had a hard enough time getting him to give the child up for a few hours to attend a party. Discouraged, she hunched forward. Resting her elbows on her knees, she held her head in her hands. "What I need is a miracle," she mumbled.

"I've seen a few."

She started. Abruptly straightening, she peered toward the front door. How had *he* come outside so quietly? "I didn't know you were still up." Why did it have to be the very man she was working so hard not to think about?

"I told you," he said. "I don't sleep."

Mary knew why she couldn't sleep and wondered what his reason was. Her curiosity would never be satisfied, however, since the last thing on earth she intended to do was ask.

"So what's the miracle?"

Her face went hot with humiliation. She hadn't meant for anyone to hear. Leaning back, she feigned calm, and lied. "I'm hoping you'll turn into a pillar of salt by daybreak."

His chuckle was less mirthful than cynical. "Oh?" She heard him approach over the redwood planks. "You'd be surprised how often I've heard that."

"I'd be less surprised than relieved." She tried to sound flip, though her heart had begun a wayward hammering. "It restores my faith in humanity."

He walked to the porch railing and lounged against it, crossing his arms at his chest. He looked yummy, to use Pauline's kitchen-romp description from the night before. Mary hadn't noticed the moon was full until its golden illumination paid subtle homage to Bonn's wide shoulders. Though his face was in shadow, moonbeams glanced off the outer reaches of his chiseled features, hinting at the sharp-edged strength of his bone structure. Frustrated by how the vision of him casually loitering there made her feel, she shifted her attention to the heavens and the calming purity of its stars.

"I thought we might have that dance, now."

His comment startled her so badly she forgot her resolve not to look at him. "Have what?"

"We promised Miz Witty."

She stared, dumbfounded that he would even make such an outrageous suggestion. "*So?*"

"So, a promise is a promise." He held out a hand as though he expected her to take it. A night breeze whispered through the branches of the evergreens. The astringent fragrance of the pines cavorted with the light perfume of Miz Witty's hybrid roses, a heady mix.

The zesty bouquet affected Mary in a most unexpected, provocative way. At least that's what she chose to believe was the cause of her shortness of breath. It certainly wasn't the vision of Bonn, standing in the half-light of night, backlit by the moon. Even motionless, he exuding a relentless charisma—with his breeze-tossed hair and dark, penetrating eyes. His extended hand seduced without the need for words, slyly compelling her to come into his arms.

Put yourself out of your misery and take his hand! a rebellious imp in her brain shouted. *You know you want to! Stand up! Walk into his embrace!* In an effort to defy the mutinous voice clamoring in her head, she clamped her fingers around the metal chair arms. "Oh? A promise is a promise, huh?" she jeered, as angry with herself as she was with him. "And you're *strict* about keeping promises?"

"Aren't you?"

She frowned, disconcerted. "Aren't I—what?"

"Strict about keeping promises to Miz Witty."

She opened her mouth to reply, then closed it. What was he doing, reminding her that she'd promised, that her promises meant something, even if his didn't? "Well—I was just—I was simply—telling her what she wanted to hear. I had no intention of actually dancing with you."

He lowered his outstretched hand to the porch railing. "I see." He canted his head, giving the moonlight greater access to his features, highlighting them to intolerable perfection. *Wicked, cruel moonlight!* "So, it's acceptable for you to tell her what she wants to hear, and not mean it, but it's reprehensible when I do it?"

"Yes!" Uncomfortably aware her response lacked logic, she scrambled mentally to correct the inconsistency. "Because—because *I'm* not hurting her when I do it!" *Ha! That told him!*

"Are you sure? She's the one who wanted us to dance."

Mary didn't appreciate feeling like she was under cross-examination. "Look, I don't care if you were captain of your fancy school's debating team, or if you think it's fun to take a subject and twist it to make your case, but the bottom line is, I don't intend to dance with you, now or *ever*." She had another thought and threw it out. "You've been in too many courtrooms listening to your lawyer's convoluted justifications for your bad behavior. It's rubbed off." She stood abruptly, intent on escape. "We're not in court, Mr. Wittering, and no matter how you spin the facts, you have no case."

"Now who's flimflamming to make her lie sound honorable?" he asked.

She halted a foot from the door. Annoyed by his truth-twisting, she whirled to face him. *"Flim-flamming? Me?"*

One broad shoulder rose and fell in silent affirmation. "It's only a dance," he said. "The last thing Miz Witty said to me after I carried her upstairs was, 'Promise me you and Mary will have that dance. Don't disappoint me.'" In the pause that followed, Mary grew uneasy. She knew he spoke the truth, since that was also the last thing Miz Witty made *her* promise before she tucked her in for the night.

"I promised her we would," he said, at last.

Mary fought her unruly desire to dance with him, promise or no promise. Every moment at the party she'd longed to be held in his arms, and she'd fought it all evening. She still yearned for it so badly she could cry, but she didn't dare weaken. She opened the front door, planning to hurry inside. Soft, sultry music wafted through the open doorway. Startled, she frowned over her shoulder at him. "You turned on the compact disc player?"

He no longer lounged against the rail, but stood close, closer than her determination to resist could withstand. How had he walked so quietly across the porch? "Dancing is nicer with music," he said, his voice beguiling in the darkness.

Darn the man! If she didn't keep herself under harsh control she might...

She made a guttural sound, banishing the mental picture of what she might do. It was certainly nothing unique, at least not for him. She imagined a hundred other foolish women like her had succumbed to the exact same fate with this man. She had to resist becoming one hundred and one! She mustn't surrender! Not even for something as innocent as a dance. She feared that once surrendering, she would not have the strength to resist—*anything* he might ask of her. Sex was a sport to him, women a challenge. She had to keep that sad reality at the forefront in her mind.

The song played on, slow and sexy. By now it was half over. Mary wanted to reject him sternly, with some pithy jab at his ego, but found herself debilitated to the point where she could hardly form words, let alone anything pithy enough to wound.

"Well...er..." She swallowed, attempting to remove the breathy squeak from her voice. Was she weakening, or facing the fact that she had a promise to keep? Though her emotions brawled, she kept her head, made a pact with herself. She would dance with him, but the dance would be brief and she would remain strong. "Okay—just to the end of this song."

"Good enough." He moved into her personal space. She felt the intrusion like static electricity, prickling all over her body. As he took her in his arms, the prickle became a pleasant tingle. *Oh, heaven! Oh, joy!* She fairly melted, her hard-fought vow of indifference taking a beating. He smelled delicious. His hand at the small of her back, radiated a pleasing heat. *No! Don't think about him!* She clamped her jaws together, stared into his shirtfront, telling herself not to notice his scent or his touch. *Be emotionally and physically detached,* she admonished silently.

To save face, she murmured, "Just so we're clear, I'm dancing with you only because I promised Miz Witty." She lifted her gaze to his face, eyeing him with a look she hoped spoke volumes about her distaste for this exercise.

Even in the deep darkness, she sensed his intent expression didn't change. Perhaps it was too dark for him to discern her rebuking look. She was afraid that wasn't it, since she was facing the moonlight and her expression would be easier to see.

His eyes glinted in the darkness, cunningly sensual, holding her gaze. ''I'm trying to be all Miz Witty could ask for in a grandson,'' he whispered, the sound of his voice washing over her like a warm, lulling wave.

Mary battled its effect without success. Anxiety gnawed at her. She was worried, restless, not breathing well. ''I must admit,'' she said, stiffly, ''tonight, your imitation of a gentleman was flawless.'' She felt suddenly disoriented. Had she said that out loud? It was a thought she hadn't meant to broadcast.

His lips parted in a crooked grin. She could see the glint of his teeth. Witnessing such a rare phenomenon as his smile, at such close range, even if it merely mocked her, was almost too much to cope with. She felt weak-kneed and breathless. ''Damning me with faint praise isn't going to get you out of this any sooner, Miss O'Mara.'' The warning came in a whisper, caressing her cheek.

The crispness of the night air, the spicy tang of his aftershave, mingling with that special zest that was utterly him, was more exhilarating, more erotic than a mortal woman could bear.

Mary tried to ignore his charisma, but floundered. At that moment in time he was all she could ask for in a man. Nothing she wanted, but all she could ask for. How crazy was that? Discouraged and resentful, she thought, *"So this is how playboys get to be playboys. They become experts at being irresistible!"*

"I thought your little sister would be at the party," he said, drawing her from her troubled reverie. She almost blessed him for giving her something to think about besides how irresistible he was. She nodded. "She was but—but Joe said she had a cold and wouldn't let her come."

"That's too bad."

She looked up, met his gaze. He was no longer smiling, and seemed sincere. "It's more than too bad," she said, her anger at Joe resurfacing. "Becca doesn't have a cold. Joe was being is usual shabby self. Keeping us apart was pure maliciousness." She swallowed, working to keep her voice from breaking. "It's cruel. Becca's looked forward to this party—for weeks."

Bonn was silent, contemplative, his expression somber. Unsettled by the provocative effect of his quiet, thoughtful side, she wrenched her gaze from his face. *Shouldn't the confounded love song be over by now?*

"Would you like me to talk to him?"

Once again, Mary was jolted from her anxiety-ridden musings by a confusing statement. ''Him? Who?''

''Becca's father,'' he said.

''Why?'' she asked. ''Do you think because your name is Wittering, you'd have some kind of power over Joe?'' She shook her head in disbelief. ''I knew you had an immense ego, but I had no idea you fancied yourself a supreme being!''

''I'm not quite that egocentric,'' he said. ''But, ego aside, I have been known to be persuasive.''

She made a pained face. ''Your reputation is no great secret. I'm sure with your charm, you could persuade almost anybody to do almost anything. But I know Joe pretty well, and I have to say he's a sliver more pigheaded than you are charming, so stay out of it. You'd only make things worse.''

He nodded. She thought she detected a muscle flex in his jaw. Had she hit a nerve? She experienced a stab of guilt. She'd been critical and severe when he'd offered to help. She supposed nobody was one hundred percent bad, including Bonn Wittering. Sucking in a breath, she said, ''Look, I'm sorry. I'm sure you meant well. It's just that Joe is a bullheaded jerk, and I'm afraid he'd just punish Becca and me, keep us apart even more, if he felt bullied—''

"I understand," he broke in, quietly. "Forget it."

His hand on her back shifted slightly, his fingers spreading. Mary sensed he'd drawn her infinitesimally closer. Their thighs brushed and she experienced a thrill. In an effort to nip her arousal in the bud, she bit down hard on her lower lip. *Now you can concentrate on the pain, nitwit,* she reprimanded inwardly, *instead of the man!*

Their dancing gradually turned them around, allowing the moon's glow to spotlight his face. Unprepared for the dramatic beauty the silvery light lavished on his ruggedly handsome features, Mary could only stare. Her pulse skyrocketing, she searched for any visible imperfection to focus on, but could find none—only bold, dark eyes and the heart-fluttering planes and angles of his face.

He looked compassionate and troubled. What she saw in his expression, so poignant in the moonglow, touched her, short-circuiting her vow to remain numb to his touch, his scent, his charisma. Her long-fought hunger to know again the taste of his kiss rushed back full-force. Her hand, resting on his shoulder, slid to his back, drawing him closer. She lifted her chin, parting her lips in a primeval invitation. Even knowing how stupid she was, how wrong this was, she couldn't stop herself. *Kiss me,* she cried inwardly. *Make love to me! Now! Before I regain my wits!*

She sensed more than saw in him a slight hesitation, a half-startled wariness, as though he couldn't quite trust her silent solicitation. Could she blame him? How often had she made it explicit that he steer clear of her? No trespassing! Touching *verboten!* Even casual conversation outside Miz Witty's presence, she'd huffily rejected. And now, in the blink of an eye, she was asking him to kiss her, offering her lips with abandon—the foolish moth fluttering carelessly into the fire. A misty doubt flitted across her mind, but it was too wispy, too swiftly banished, to weigh or heed.

Suddenly they were kissing, Mary's wordless, witless request granted. His kiss was tender, like his first, still burning in her memory. The touch of his lips was unlike anything she'd expected a selfish, egotistical good-for-nothing's kiss to be. The taste and texture was truly heaven on earth, exactly as she remembered. Her toes curled, her body quivered and she had the strangest sensation she no longer stood on solid ground. She fairly floated like some airy, scudding cloud, but not nearly as cool. She felt warm. *Hot,* even.

Seeming to sense she had arrived at the brink of total surrender, Bonn's tongue teased her lips, subtly claiming mastery of the secret recesses of her mouth. She abandoned herself to his sweet sovereignty as he explored and stimulated.

Wanting more, much more, she molded every curve of her body to his. She could feel his powerful, male hardness against her. Heat, wild and fierce, spread through her veins, filling her with a throbbing need—mindless and wanton and wonderful.

A part of her, the logical part she'd ruthlessly shoved aside, protested, but the part of her that sizzled, trembled, craving deep intimacy, drove logic and intellect back with bulldozer determination.

Desolate and terrified that what she was about to do would cause her damage that couldn't heal, her rational side screamed, pleading, protesting, reminding her she'd only managed to lure him here with her threat that Miz Witty would cut him out of her will. This man, with the sexy-yet-tender kiss and deceptively sincere eyes, was the same money-grubbing snake he'd been before his arrival.

Even with all his broad-shouldered gorgeousness and that rare, mind-melting grin, he was a self-centered rogue. In the midst of her mindless tailspin, even as she reveled in the lusty joys of his scent, his lips, the hard strength of his broad back beneath her fingers, his bold maleness and the promise of dazzling gratification to come, her reason battled back, recapturing its rightful dominance.

What in heaven's name are you doing, Mary?

Horrified at herself for such an abysmal mental slide, she shoved at his chest, crying wretchedly, "If you think getting into my pants will do you any good with Miz Witty, you're mistaken! My opinion won't change! But," she admitted brokenly, "...you've probably—succeeded in what you came to do, so—so making love to me is a chore you can avoid!" She knew how absurd that sounded, considering who had initiated the kiss, but she couldn't let herself admit that. It was too awful to think about.

She stumbled away, only halted in her blind retreat by the porch rail. Instinctively, she grabbed it to keep from toppling into the ornamental plantings.

She heard an exhale from behind her that carried the growled undertone of a curse. "I feel a case of whiplash coming on," he muttered, sounding hoarse. "How about you?"

She supposed she deserved that, considering her abrupt about-face from "make love to me" to "stay out of my pants"! Her U-turn had been so violent, it was enough to cause physical injury. Dizzy and disoriented, she faced away from him, leaning heavily on the rail to keep from collapsing. "I'm—fine." She squeezed her eyes shut, condemning herself to the deepest pit in Hades.

How could she have done anything so stupid? She knew better!

Ordinarily she was a crisp, clear-headed logical thinker. But right now her thinking was muddled and contradictory. Her goals—at least where Bonn Wittering was concerned—had scattered like defecting cowards, and she was tottering on the edge of hysteria.

Shaken and angry over her lapse, she pulled herself together as well as she could, ordering her voice and her pulse to settle down. "You know, Mr. Wittering—you're *awfully* good," she said. "I'm impressed as—as *heck.*"

There was a pause, so long she wondered if he'd gone inside. If he had, he hadn't shut the door. She could still hear the music.

"Heck, huh?" he said, finally. "That's pretty strong language. I'm curious to know what you're so impressed about."

She refused to face him. That was unwise, even if she hadn't been so mortified she didn't think she'd ever be able to look him directly in the eyes again. "You've perfected the New Alpha Male icon. Women can't resist it." Quiet filled the night and she strained to hold on to her fragile poise.

"If you don't mind," he said, "I'll reserve judgment on your flattery before I say thanks." The plaintive sound of an owl invaded the lull, its melancholy outcry dying away before he spoke again. "Just what is a New Alpha Male?"

She inhaled, gaining both emotional and physical strength. Not looking at him helped. "It's the same as the old Alpha Male, the status thing— money, power—but with sensitivity thrown in." She shook her head, befuddled. "The only thing is, the sensitivity is supposed to be real. And I swear, sometimes when I look into your eyes, I actually believe…"

Simmering hysteria edged toward the surface again, and she laughed aloud. How foolish could she be? Any sensitivity she thought she saw in his eyes was part of his act. "I guess all *really* successful playboys have that gift. For a minute there, you even had *me* going!" She ground her teeth, determined to mean what she was about to say. "And *I* can't stand you."

"But you like me better than my lawyer, right?"

She didn't see how that could possibly matter, but she saw no reason to deny it. "It's a toss-up, but yes, I suppose I do—barely."

His response was a mirthless chuckle. "Thanks," he said, his tone edged with cynicism. "Is there an antivenom for that poison dart, or do I just stand here until everything goes black?"

"Stand wherever you please! I don't care!" The wrought-up quiver in her voice hinted broadly that she wasn't as indifferent as she wanted to be.

Headlights hit them straight-on as a car turned off the blacktop road beyond the border of evergreens. It approached along Miz Witty's long, meandering drive. Mary squinted as the vehicle crept forward, its high beams lighting up landscaped berms, splashing ghostly plantings with brief bursts of color. The sound of tires crunching over gravel seemed overloud, magnified in the stillness. "Who in the world…" Mary wondered aloud, but let the sentence drop.

"Maybe somebody forgot something."

Mary supposed that was possible. "How important could it be for them to come back for it now?"

"Isn't it lucky we're up?" he muttered, derisively.

She straightened, removing one supporting hand from the railing to shade her eyes. "That's one way of putting it."

The car pulled to a stop beside Bonn's rental, the headlights blessedly extinguished along with the engine. Once again, the world was dark and quiet, but something in the cosmos had lurched out of alignment. What it was, Mary couldn't quite put her finger on.

The driver's side door of the newcomer's car opened and someone got out. Though Mary's night vision had been impaired by the headlights' glare, she wasn't kept in suspense long about what sex their late-night visitor was.

"Well, well," a female voice called, "I never expected a welcoming committee at two-thirty in the morning."

The stranger approached the front steps. Mary could see her better. She was tall, slender and around thirty, in a trim, light-colored business suit. Her hair was short and equally light-colored. As she mounted the steps, she waved and smiled—at Bonn. Her face had become visible enough in the moon's glow to reveal exceptional beauty.

Mary clutched the rail. Her adrenaline level shot up in a fight or flight response. Bewildered and disconcerted, she couldn't imagine why she felt a need to do both?

"Bonn, *baby!*" The striking female extended her arms as though she anticipated being swept into his embrace. *"Surprise, surprise!"*

CHAPTER EIGHT

TAGGART couldn't believe his eyes. Lee Stanton stepped onto the porch and strutted toward him as though she expected him to react with a lusty lunge at her. *Blast it!* That's all he needed, an ex-lover with no intention of remaining an ex, showing up now!

At least she'd remembered to call him Bonn.

Not surprisingly, she waltzed up to him, slid her arms about his neck and planted a kiss on his lips. Not a "Hi-it's-nice-to-see-you" kiss, but an "I'm-hot-for-you-where's-the-bed?" kiss. He rested his hands on her upper arms, pressing her away. "Hello, Lee." Indicating Mary, who finally turned to face him, he said, "Meet Mary O'Mara, Miz Witty's caregiver. Mary, this is Lee Stanton. A—friend from Boston."

Unsmiling, Mary shifted her gaze from Taggart to the clinging woman. "How do you do, Miss Stanton," she said, without inflection.

Lee didn't completely release Taggart's neck, but loosened her grasp enough to shift around to look at Mary. "Oh—hello, there," she said.

Taggart could tell Lee found Mary insignificant. Lee came from wealth and privilege. The trait he disliked most about her was her superior attitude when she addressed people she felt were beneath her, which included all household staffers, office clerks, paralegals. Even junior partners in the law firm. "You will excuse us," she said with a low, suggestive laugh. "But it's been several days since I've seen—Bonn."

Taggart couldn't help watching Mary's face. Her features carried a startling lack of information. The point of her tongue slowly moistened her lower lip and Taggart felt a rush of heat infuse his body. The night breeze told him his forehead had broken out in a sweat. How could she do that? Lee just kissed him, and he felt nothing. But watching Mary O'Mara moisten her lip with the scant tip of her tongue, his skin felt singed and he struggled for breath like a man suffering from smoke inhalation.

Drawing her lips in a tight smile, Mary planted her fists on her hips. "Don't mind me. I'm getting used to seeing women hang on him like gold chains."

"Really?" Lee eyed him with skepticism. He wasn't surprised she found that remark hard to believe. After all, she knew Taggart for the conservative workaholic he was. She'd been with the law firm of Baxter, Barker and Lancaster for four years before she'd moved up to full partner three years ago. Lee was well aware Taggart worked twelve hour days and had little time to meet women, let alone have affairs with them. His lack of free time had undoubtedly been the major reason he'd begun the affair with her.

It had been a mistake he was still paying for.

"Well, well, Bonn, I leave you alone for a few days and you've already spun your bad-boy web over all the Rocky Mountain maidens?"

Dragging his gaze from Mary, he frowned at Lee. "Not all of them."

"Tell me, Mr. Wittering," Mary asked, her tone scornful. "Do you kiss *every* female you meet?"

He experienced a stab in his gut, unsure why. Looking wearily from one woman to the other, he felt like a criminal, condemned for a crime he didn't commit. "No, I don't kiss every female I meet." His gaze slid back to Mary. He hadn't initiated either kiss on that front porch, and she damn well knew it. "Sometimes they kiss me."

"Look, Marsha, be a good girl and fetch my bags," Lee said, smiling at Taggart. He could feel her lace her fingers at the back of his neck, connecting herself to him like a noose. "They're in the trunk. I'm simply too exhausted."

Yeah, right, Taggart thought. *If that sultry purr I hear in your voice is exhaustion, I'll eat your baggage.* He reached up and disengaged her hold on him. "I'll get the suitcases, Lee. *Mary* is Miz Witty's caregiver, not yours." He slung a controlling arm about the blonde's shoulders, guiding her off the porch and down the steps, planning to have a private word with her. "Why don't you come, too."

She giggled. The sexy sound used to turn him on. Now it annoyed the fire out of him. "I love it when you talk dirty," she whispered, but Taggart feared it had not been quiet enough to keep Mary from overhearing. When they reached the trunk, he opened it, masking himself and Lee from Mary's view. "What the hell are you doing here?" he ground out under his breath. "Who's minding the store?"

"Don't worry, *Daddy,*" she teased, sounding more amused than sympathetic. "I know, I know, Baxter and Barker are both four hundred years old, but they're not dead. They manage to hobble into the office on occasion. And when they don't, they can be reached on the golf course. Otherwise, the children can handle things."

To Lee, all lawyers in the firm beneath the level of "partner" were "the children." She even called them that to their faces. She wasn't the most popular lawyer in the firm, but she had a razor-sharp mind and was lethal in court, and that's what counted.

"Dammit, Lee, this pretense is hard enough to sustain without..." He tried to be polite. Old habits died hard. "...without complications."

She slid an arm about his waist, squeezing possessively. "Don't panic—Bonn. See, I've been practicing all the way from the airport. Besides, I brought some papers that need your signature."

"Oh? I hadn't heard the United States Post Office, Federal Express and UPS had all folded."

"Funny man." She playfully poked him in the ribs. "Actually, I was thinking. You know, about how you needed a vacation. And I decided I did, too. So I thought a few days in the Rockies would be just the ticket."

"You thought wrong."

She indicated her suitcases. "Aren't you going to get them?"

"No," he said. "You're not staying."

Her expression changed from giggly girlfriend to tough-as-nails lawyer. "Of course, I am. Don't be ridiculous."

"Me? Ridiculous?" Her lack of sensitivity amazed him. "You show up, unannounced, at the home of a total stranger, in the middle of the night and you expect—"

"That's not my fault," she cut in. "I tried to call you. Where is your cell?"

"It's in a drawer, turned off," he said. "After that call you made, I decided it was too chancy to keep it with me. Besides, I'm on vacation, remember?''

''Well, I'm here, and I'm staying.'' She nudged him provocatively with her hip. ''I don't need a room—just half your bed.''

From the moment he'd recognized her when she'd stepped out of her rental car, he'd known this was coming. Resentment at her assumption that they would be sleeping together raged through him. ''Not a chance, Lee,'' he said. ''I'm supposed to be here entertaining my frail, old grandmother, not for a sex-fest with you.''

He was angry, and it was hard to keep his voice low, but he made himself. ''Miz Witty may not be my grandmother, but I like her. I won't have this supposed reunion tainted. I won't let her think her beloved Bonny couldn't keep his zipper shut for a two week visit with his only living relative. *Confound it,* Lee, the woman adores Bonn. She thinks I'm him. I won't corrupt what could be her last memory of him by having her think he'd rather…'' Taggart was worn out from the strain of putting a polite spin on his words. He decided to say what he felt. ''…have meaningless sex.''

She blinked, but otherwise he could detect no emotional hit. What did he expect? She was cast iron. It made her a great defense lawyer, but not necessarily a great human being. To benefit her client's cause in court, she could ruthlessly dirty a victim's reputation and never feel a twinge of remorse.

With an exasperated exhale, he went on. "Who knows when or if Bonner's grandmother will ever see him again. If he goes to jail, she could die before he gets out. If that happens, then these two weeks have to be the best I can make them for her. Surely you can see that."

Lee blinked again, glanced away and pursed her lips. He didn't think she had it in her to be regretful or apologetic, but something about the action made him feel this was as close as she would ever get. Even when judges threatened her with contempt of court, her apologies sounded more like "Go To Hades!" than true repentance.

She touched his arm. "Good grief, Taggart," she said, "I had no idea you'd take this little prank so seriously."

He turned away, stared up at the sky. Before he'd met Miz Witty, he hadn't thought about how the impersonation would affect her. He'd only been thinking of Bonn's predicament, and how much he owed his friend. "It was never a prank to me," he muttered. "I was angry at first, but now…" He shook his head. "Miz Witty's a nice woman," he said. "I won't hurt her and I don't intend to give you the chance to, either." He frowned. "Your being here makes it twice as likely one of us will forget the ruse at the wrong moment and break that lonely woman's heart.''

Lee eyed him with disbelief. ''You sound like you really care.''

''*Hell,* Lee, what have I been saying?''

She shook her head and perched on the edge of the car trunk. ''Well, that's positively quaint, baby. But say what you will, and feel what you will, I'm not leaving. My return flight out of Denver is next Wednesday. So all I can do is promise I'll be on my best behavior.'' She glanced up at his face. ''In public.'' She took his hand, smiling. ''This is a new side to you, Tag.'' She squeezed his fingers. ''Maybe it's a mental abnormality brought on by breathing thin mountain air, but I've never seen you so passionate about not wanting to hurt somebody's feelings.'' She raised his hand to her cheek, rubbing his knuckles along her skin. ''It's very sexy.''

He rolled his eyes, tugging from her grip. ''Yeah, you're off to a great start, Miss Best Behavior.''

''I said, in public,'' she reminded. Standing, she smoothed her slim skirt. ''You get the bags— *Bonn,* baby—and I'll let the nursemaid show me to a room of my own. Surely there must be something in that big place.''

''*Damnation,* Lee!'' Her condescension toward Mary grated on him as much as her bullheaded-ness. "Go back to Boston. Your being here will not change what I said in March. How many times do I have to break it off?" He hoped his bluntness would force her to realize what she wanted to be rekindled between them would never happen.

She crossed her arms before her, looking immovable on the subject. "Okay, fine! I'll go, but before I do, don't be surprised if I blow your whole charade—*Taggart Lancaster!*" Her expression and her tone was hard. "Do I make myself abundantly clear?"

He wasn't unduly surprised. Disappointed, but not surprised. Lee was a top litigator, and top litigators could be merciless. He should know. There had been times in his career when he'd shown no mercy, either. As things stood now, he didn't have any recourse but to believe her threat. If it were just him, he wouldn't care. But he wasn't going to hurt Miz Witty. Not for anything.

There was another reason, too. One he didn't like to think about—didn't want to acknowledge. But it was there, hovering around the edges of his mind. The idea of leaving now, never to see Mary again, caused him actual physical pain. He took a deep breath, trying to discipline his temper and his stubborn heart. "So, it's blackmail?" he demanded stonily.

She smiled, looking like her old, crafty self. "Let's not call it blackmail, baby."

"That's what it is."

She rested her hands on his shoulders and pecked his cheek. "I know, but let's not call it that." Indicating her bags, she added, "Now that that's settled, you get the suitcases."

"You don't care that I've made it clear there's nothing between us?"

Her laughter was husky, as though he'd said something absurdly naive. "Men. You're all alike. You don't know what you know until the right woman tells you." She patted his cheek. "Be a good boy, baby, and get my bags."

He stared her down. The censure in his expression made no impression. She puckered as though throwing him a kiss. "I'll ask Magda to show me to a room."

"Her name is Mary," he gritted, dragging out the first bag. "Mary O'Mara. It's not a difficult name to remember."

She turned away. Without looking back, she said, "Mary? Magda? Who cares?"

As he hauled out the second suitcase, he peered at Lee's retreating form. "I do," he muttered, then cringed at hearing his answer stated aloud. It had hardly been a wild, over-the-top declaration of love. Nevertheless he felt like a traitor.

When Mary surprised him with her kiss on the porch, stopping himself from dragging her down to the bare boards and making love to her had been hell on wheels. He didn't want to feel that much heat for anybody. What was it about Mary that caused such a restless, impatient and unruly effect on him? Something—a flash of inspiration, an inkling of inescapable truth—tried to bubble up from his subconscious, but he resisted, rejected it. He wasn't ready, refused to face it.

"Dammit!" His curse, raw with pain and self-disgust, was masked by the slam of the trunk. Bowing his head as though in prayer, he rested the flats of his hands on the trunk and slouched forward, weary and heartsick. Memories of his lost love assailed him. Memories that had sustained him these past five years. He'd thought they would always be enough. "I'm so sorry, Annalisa," he whispered, guilt riding him hard. "Tell me what to do."

So this was the woman Bonner Wittering cared about. For some reason, Mary found herself disappointed in the man for his taste. There was no arguing that Lee Stanton was striking, most likely a high-fashion model. But she seemed—hard, somehow. And completely self-absorbed.

Mary moved slowly down the stairs from the second floor, this new development monopolizing her thoughts. She shook her head at herself for feeling the slightest bit depressed. "Why are you surprised?" she mumbled. "He's a gorgeous, selfish jerk. Why shouldn't his girlfriend be a gorgeous, selfish jerkette? Look at it logically. They're perfect for each other." Sadly, Mary found it hard to look at anything logically that pertained to Bonner Wittering. That was her whole trouble.

She heard the front door open and lifted her gaze to see the blonde come inside.

"Oh, there you are," Lee said, placing a well-manicured hand on one slim hip. "I'll need a room." She arched a brow, looking highly put out. "Bonner thinks it would upset granny if we sleep together." Mary was surprised that Bonn had insisted on separate rooms. Maybe he did have a little sensitivity in his soul, after all.

Waving toward the upstairs, Lee added, "I'd prefer something with southern exposure."

Mary had a hard time holding back the suggestion that Miss High-And-Mighty turn around, and she'd be happy to boot her precious southern exposure out onto the gravel. She managed a polite smile, and counted to ten.

On the off-off chance Bonn's girlfriend would need a room, Mary had gone up to ask Ruby about the only other one available, in the old carriage house, now the garage. The second level had been turned into a charming guest room with bath, but Mary hadn't been sure if it was ready for occupancy. Groggy and affronted, Ruby told her it was *always* ready.

"I'll show you to your room," she murmured. Walking past the woman, Mary flipped a switch that turned on the light illuminating the outside stairway that led up to the carriage house guest room. "If you'll follow me." Mary opened the front door.

"What? *Outside?*" the blonde asked, her tone critical.

Once again Mary had an urge to say something that might be construed as inelegant. She swallowed the impulse and nodded. "The room over the garage is quite lovely. Really our best—with wonderful southern exposure." She indicated outside. "It's only a few steps from the main house."

Mary led the way onto the porch in time to see Bonn, a suitcase in each fist, come to a halt at the bottom of the porch steps. His attention had been drawn to the light Mary turned on. When her footfalls sounded on the redwood planks, his glance shifted to her. "Is that the room?" he asked.

Mary nodded. "It's quite nice."

"I'm sure it is," he said as the blonde joined Mary on the porch.

"I'm afraid the only other guest room in the house is tiny, and the bed is a junior size." Mary wasn't sure why she felt the need to make excuses, but she hurried on. "It's little Becca's room, when she visits."

"No need to explain," Bonn said. "Lee will be perfectly comfortable." He glanced at the blonde, his expression unreadable, even bathed in moonlight. "Won't you?"

Lee didn't speak at once, but crossed the porch to the stairs. Her high heels making sharp, harsh clicks. "Of course, baby," she said, descending the steps to meet him.

Though Mary could no longer see the blonde's face, a smile lilted in her voice. She certainly hadn't smiled at Mary when they'd been inside. The newcomer saved her friendliness for the only audience that mattered to her.

Bonner Wittering.

"Breakfast is served in the kitchen around—"

"Don't bother running over the house rules," the blonde called without taking her eyes off her tall, handsome companion. "Bonner can—fill me in."

Mary experienced a twinge at the blatant sexual innuendo. "Yes, well…" She cleared a rusty quiver from her throat, watched the woman take his arm, then decided staring longingly after such an unworthy man was a criminal waste of energy. "Good night."

Neither answered, seemingly lost in gazing into each other's eyes. Mary went inside, closed the door and was halfway up the stairs before she noticed the compact disc player still gushed out sexy love songs. She tramped back down the stairs, turned off the music, then stomped up to her room. *Let him stare into her eyes all night if he wants to! Let him make wild, noisy love to her until they both pass out from dehydration! It's nothing to me! Nothing at all.*

Alone in her room, she trudged to her bed and fell forward, too exhausted and desolate to do anything else. "Let them howl at the moon like animals. *I don't care,*" she whispered brokenly, "Please—just let me sleep, and don't let me dream about—about his kiss."—

Mary did drop off to sleep, but not for long. She woke up with a start, facing the fact that she must brush her teeth, take off her sneakers and change out of her sweater and jeans. A bath would be nice, too, warm and relaxing. She didn't expect Bonn back soon, if at all. He was no doubt *filling in* his company! Mary sat up and covered her face with her hands. Ugh! No good would come from visualizing that!

She went to her dresser and pulled out her nightgown and headed for the bathroom. Inside, she switched on the overhead light, then flinched at its brightness. Deciding to bathe in candlelight, she lit the lavender-scented candle on the glass shelf above the sink. She kept it there for nights like this, when her stress level skyrocketed—as it did every time Joe Lukins refused to keep a promise to Becca.

She hung her nightgown on the hook on her door, extinguished the overhead light, set the stopper in the tub drain and turned on the water. After doffing her clothes and folding them neatly on a chair, she swirled her hair up on top of her head and secured it with a large clip before stepping into the old-fashioned, claw-footed tub.

She lounged back to relax. Several minutes later, the tub brimmed with restorative, steamy water. She turned off the flow and lay back for a cathartic soak. Utterly still and dimly lit, the bathroom became a soothing, lavender-scented haven, where cares could be cleansed from her mind, at least for a time.

She inhaled deeply, taking in the pleasant aroma, then exhaled slowly, expelling the hurts and anxieties of the day. She concentrated on breathing slowly in and out. In and out. This calming exercise helped ease her tensions, purged her mind, and—she fervently hoped—would allow her to finally fall into a restful sleep.

Eyes closed, she breathed in the soothing scent until she began to drift along in a state of half consciousness, her weary body and overburdened mind transported to another plane of existence. A softer, gentler place where people like Joe Lukins and Bonner Wittering didn't exist.

Somewhere, sometime, floating along in her toasty, slumberous cocoon, Mary had the oddest dream. A man stood over her, still and quiet. Then out of the utter stillness, she heard him speak a word. She jerked at the quarrelsome, bitten-off sound of it. Not a happy word. What was such an unhappy word doing in her quiet, gentle place?

In her half-sleeping state, she lolled her head back and forth, trying to fine tune her dream. She became aware of another sound, vaguely grating, like the screeching of metal scraping against metal, intermingled with the rustle of something. Fabric? She yawned and wriggled, willing the abrasive noise away.

She heard a click, as though a door had quietly closed. She blinked, now more awake than asleep. Inhaling, she stretched. That had been such a curious dream, with a strange combination of impressions. Having dozed off, she knew she should get to bed while she was in this deliciously drowsy state. She sat up, stretched again, but this time her hand brushed something. She glanced toward the outside of the tub, perplexed. A few seconds slipped by before she gathered enough of her sleepy wits to realize the faded, white lace curtain that hung from the metal rod encircling the old tub, had been drawn. She glanced toward the candle, now only a gauzy bit of off-white light visible through the fabric and plastic liner.

She rubbed her eyes, puzzled. She hadn't drawn the curtain. She knew that for a fact, because she remembered being able to see the candle quite clearly before—

Oh, Lord in Heaven!

She was jarred starkly awake, mortified to the depth of her soul. It hadn't been a dream! *He* had barged right in! He'd seen her in the tub. Stretched out—*naked!*

A sound issued up from her throat, a half whimper, half groan. Reflexively, she drew herself up in a ball of humiliation. How dare he charge in without knocking? How dare he stand there, staring down at her—so defenseless and—and so *exposed!* Furious at his audacity, and already as shamed as it was possible to be, she shouted, "Mr. Wittering, next time let's think about *knocking,* shall we?"

He didn't respond.

She flung back the curtain and climbed out, grabbed a towel and wrapped herself in it. "All right, let's just get into it!" she muttered, too mad to allow logic or reason to intercede. She knocked loudly on the door that led to his bedroom. "Mr. Wittering? Did you hear me?" she called, determined to confront him for his inexcusable ogling. "Answer me! I know you're in there!"

The doorknob rattled. She jumped back as he pushed open the door. He loomed before her, bare-chested, motionless in the bath's entry. No lamps were lit in his room, though moonlight streamed in the front window. Nature's nightlight was too far away to be of much value, as far as seeing him. Unfortunately for Mary, the flickering candlelight reached out, highlighting his solemn features and his chest in its mellow glow. He still wore his slacks, but no shoes. Silently, he scanned her meager attire. A muscle quivered in his jaw. Before he met her gaze, he cleared his throat. "I'm sorry," he said, simply, grimly.

When he said nothing more, she bristled. "Oh, you're *sorry,* huh?"

His eyes reflected candlelight, hampering her ability to read them. Was he repentant or merely irked at being caught? He muttered something under his breath that sounded a little like, "Sorrier than you know," but she couldn't be sure. He might have been clearing his throat. "I didn't realize you were..." His sentence died. Nostrils flaring, his jaw moved from side to side, as though he were agitated. "You looked like you were asleep."

"I thought I was," she retorted. "But my dream turned out to be a living nightmare."

A shadow of emotion fleetingly twisted his features. "The light wasn't on," he said. "How was I supposed to know you were in there?"

That was true. It had been dark. He'd probably assumed she was in bed. Speaking of being in bed, why wasn't he in the blonde's? "What time is it?" she asked.

He seemed surprised by the subject change but glanced at his wristwatch. "Three-fifteen. Why?"

"I thought it was a lot later." Apparently she had hardly dozed at all. And if that were true, then he hadn't spent much time with his ladylove, if any. She eyed him suspiciously. "Either you're not the lover you're cracked up to be or you didn't…" She wasn't sure how to finish that statement so she decided not to try. "Never mind." She shook her head to get her brain in gear. *Remember why you're standing here, in a towel, for heaven's sake! You're mad at him! Tell him!*

She readjusted her expression to proclaim her righteous indignation. "I just wanted to say—I can understand how you might have thought I was in bed and walked into the bathroom. But what I can't excuse is that you hung around to leer at me when I was so—so vulnerable! That was vile and—I'm not letting you get away with it!''

He continued to frown, but one eyebrow went up in a questioning way. ''What are you going to do, ram hot pokers in my eyes?''

''What?'' It was hard to remain coherent when she was so close to him. His naked chest, so cleverly glorified in flickering candlelight, didn't help matters.

''Would blinding me satisfy your injured pride?''

She glared, grasping his meaning. ''Don't you dare mock me!''

He shoved a hand through his hair. ''Look, I said I'm sorry.''

His troubled expression was as unnerving at it was breathtaking. Her emotions tumbled over each other, struggling for supremacy. She wasn't sure which would win out, fiery resentment or heart-pounding awe.

''It's not much of an excuse,'' he said, ''but I'm a man. When a man sees a naked woman, he reacts in a primitive way. Of course, I looked.'' His tone was flinty, almost impatient. She could feel his brooding tension electrifying the air between them. He was as angry as she was. How dare he be as angry as she! He wasn't the injured party here! ''It's involuntary, like blinking,'' he said. ''I didn't leer at you—at least no longer than

I was genetically wired to. I left as soon as I could—physically.''

She glowered at him, flabbergasted by his defense. ''So your defense is genetic *wiring?*'' she scoffed. ''Have you used that one in court yet?''

''Not personally, no,'' he said.

''Well, don't despair.'' She felt her towel slipping, so she hooked her thumbs behind the terry at her breasts, hiking it higher. ''I'm sure it's in your future.''

His gaze followed the movement of her hands readjusting her towel and his jaw muscles bulged. ''Look, I've apologized,'' he ground out. ''From now on I'll knock, whether I see a light or not. What more can I say?''

She didn't know. Why didn't she shut the door? Why could she only stand there staring at him, experiencing a wrenching sadness?

They stood on opposite sides of a terrible gulf—between morality and amorality, truth and lies, trust and betrayal. Why did her heart grieve for a bridge across the chasm? There was no bridge. There shouldn't be—at least not one that could lead her across to him. On his side there could be no happy endings.

Indicating the bathroom with a curt wave, he said, ''I'd like to take a shower, so if you could cut the lecture short…''

He was right. She'd had her say. They were both cross, both exhausted. There was nothing left to do but run as fast as she could in the opposite direction. "Give me five minutes to brush my teeth and you can have the bathroom." She spun to go.

"By the way," he said. "I didn't."

She shifted back, confused. "Didn't what?"

He slipped his hands into his slacks pockets. The flickering light was dim but not too dim to mask the sexy shift and play of muscle in his arms and chest. "Nothing." He shook his head. "Goodnight."

As she tried to break the spell the candlelit vision of his upper torso had on her ability to move, his meaning became clear. He was referring back to her comment about how little time he'd spent *filling in* his blonde. "Oh, right. I get it." Refocusing on her anger, she canted her chin upward a notch. Defiant. "Naturally, that's what you would *say*."

She stepped backward into the bathroom and slammed the door in his face.

When the world grew silent again, Mary felt strangely defeated. She walked to the pedestal sink and leaned heavily against it. Squeezing her eyes shut, she experiencing a hot, sickening rush of misery. She'd thought her slap at his sexual prowess would make her feel smug, take away some of the sting of her humiliation and heartache.

It didn't.

CHAPTER NINE

SATURDAY morning, Mary sat at the kitchen table eating breakfast. She hadn't seen Lee Stanton at all on Friday. It seemed the new arrival had been stricken with a migraine and remained huddled, moaning in her darkened bedroom, allegedly on the verge of death. Mary kept herself busy with Miz Witty's needs, but she'd heard Ruby and Pauline grumbling about Lee's whining and dictatorial orders.

"Who does she think she is?" Pauline asked, drawing Mary from her thoughts. "The Queen of *Egypt?*"

Mary ate a spoonful of her oatmeal to mask her amusement, deciding not to suggest Pauline might have meant the Queen of England. Clearly the cook was annoyed with Bonner's highfalutin girlfriend.

Mary looked at Pauline, who stood with her back to the stove. "What's she done now?" she asked.

Pauline fisted her hands on her hips. "I haven't even met her and I already hate her. She just called on the house line, saying she's coming over for breakfast in *ten* minutes and she wants a low-fat, whole wheat muffin, black coffee and fat-free vanilla yogurt with fresh strawberries!'' Pauline eyed the ceiling in high dudgeon. ''Does she expect me to wave a wand and *presto,* all that stuff will appear? This ain't no hotel!''

Mary sipped her coffee then set down the mug. ''Why don't you serve her some wheat toast and coffee and give her a choice of cereals. Doesn't Crunchyberry come with dehydrated strawberries?''

Pauline snorted, clenching her fist as though about to punch somebody. ''I'll give her a choice—of a left-handed or right-handed knuckle sandwich!'' She walked to the table and braced her fists on the surface, leaning toward Mary. ''I know this Lee woman is Bonn's girlfriend. You know, the one he *cares* about and all, but…'' She glanced toward the door making sure they were alone. ''My personal opinion is, that female is a snotty witch!'' She bent closer and dropped her voice. ''I gotta say, I think Mr. Wittering could do better.''

Mary smiled wanly and shook her head. ''No. Mr. Wittering is right where he should be, as far as girlfriends go. Neither he nor Miss Stanton are worth much as—human beings. Don't let them upset you.''

''No wonder my ears were burning.''

At the sound of Bonner's voice, Mary and Pauline jerked to stare toward the kitchen entry. Mary's heart leapt to her throat. She'd managed to avoid being around him on Friday, but a mere day, a paltry twenty-four hours, was not enough time to get over their night-time confrontation in the bath. The very thought gave her breathing problems. She concentrated on taking long, slow breaths so she wouldn't hyperventilate.

"Oh, cripes!" The cook abruptly straightened, her face going crimson. Mary felt sorry for her, obviously horrified that he'd overheard.

Though Mary tried to follow her own advice not to let him upset her, her cheeks burned, too. Unhappily, it was one thing to give advice, and another to put it to good use, especially when every foolish fiber of her being came to goofy, gaga attention when he was around.

"I should think your ears would burn all the time, Mr. Wittering," she murmured, focusing on her bowl of oatmeal. His good looks, even un-smiling, did shameful, disturbing things to her. "Surely your lifestyle generates enough gossip to keep both your ears burning—kind of like the playboy's eternal flame."

His chuckle held a trace of amusement. That startled her, but she didn't dare look at him. She feared his smile. "That should be two flames, shouldn't it?'' he asked. ''Or do you see my whole head on fire?''

She spooned up more oatmeal and ate it, refusing to respond. It was easier to keep from looking at him if she didn't speak to him.

''Mr. Wittering, sir...'' Pauline began, hesitantly, her demeanor completely unlike her initial, saucy attitude toward him. Her flannel shirt was buttoned up, showing nary a scrap of red underwear. Mary had a feeling Jed's influence had accomplished the transformation. Plainly a shy man's honest affection could bring about radical changes in a woman's overt sexuality. ''Your—um—friend, Lee, wants stuff for breakfast I don't have on hand,'' she said, glumly. ''I can buy it and have it ready tomorrow morning, but—''

''Don't worry, Pauline.'' Bonn took a seat kitty-corner from Mary. ''Lee will eat whatever you've prepared. And please, call me Bonn.''

''Yes, sir—uh—okay.'' Pauline turned toward the stove. ''There's blueberry waffles or scrambled eggs or both, and toast. And oatmeal. Plus orange juice and coffee, like usual.''

''How about some of everything,'' he said.

''Comin' up.'' The cook busied herself at the stove.

The click of high heels attracted Mary's attention and she knew immediately who had arrived. The Queen of Egypt. She turned toward the kitchen entry to offer the tall, willowy blonde a polite smile. She tried to make the expression genuine, but it felt tight. "Good morning, Miss Stanton. I trust your headache is better?"

The woman walked straight to Bonn, whose back was to the kitchen door, placed her hands on his shoulders and bent to nibble his earlobe. "Morning, baby."

"Good morning, Lee." Bonn angled his head away from her love bite, stood and faced her. "Feeling better?"

She nodded, though her expression grew theatrically tormented. "Finally!"

"That's good." He moved to the chair opposite Mary and held it out. "Join us?"

Lee took the seat, then patted his cheek. "Thanks, *Bonn.*" She smiled cryptically, and Mary couldn't fathom what the look or the emphasis on his name could mean. Some kind of lover's private joke, no doubt.

"You're welcome." He seated himself, and Mary thought she saw a hardening along his jawline. That didn't make sense, either. "By the way, Lee," he said, "Pauline isn't a short-order cook, so you get what's offered for breakfast, or you don't have to eat. Your choice." He glanced at her and smiled. "I recommend her delicious waffles."

Mary experienced a sizzle in her gut at the sight of his smile, and shifted her attention to her bowl.

"I'm not up to waffles," Lee said. There was a pause in the conversation. Mary ate her oatmeal and sipped her coffee, keeping focused on her breakfast. "Just black coffee." Lee sounded put out. "I can't keep trim eating all that *fatty* food."

"Why not have some oatmeal?" Mary glanced at her. "And skim milk. Oatmeal lowers cholesterol."

Lee waved off the idea as though it were a bothersome horsefly. "It tastes like cardboard, too."

Pauline plunked a mug of black coffee before Lee. "Here you go, ma'am." She made a face over Lee's head that only Mary caught. To mask her wayward chuckle, Mary coughed behind her hand as the cook set another mug in front of Bonn, this time with less sloshing. "And yours, sir."

"Thanks, Pauline. And, remember, it's not sir."

"Oh, yeah." She pivoted toward the stove. "Your breakfast's coming right up, Mr. Wittering."

"I'm Bonn, and there's no rush."

"Yes, sir."

Mary's glance skittered to his face. His jaw muscles bunched and jerked, his expression serious. She hurriedly dragged her attention back to her own breakfast. Why did he have to draw her like a magnet!

"Sleep well, baby?" Lee asked.

Mary experienced a surge of unruly annoyance. Unable to help herself, she quipped, "Just fine, darling." She looked at Lee with as much innocence as she could muster. "Or—weren't you talking to me?"

Bonn chuckled, the rich sound filling the kitchen. Mary was startled she'd been able to make him laugh, considering how solemn he'd looked seconds ago. She wanted badly to search his face, look into his eyes, but forced herself to keep focused on Lee.

The woman eyed Mary, her expression a blend of speculation and disdain. After a moment, she shifted her attention to Bonn and smiled broadly. It was as though Mary had never spoken and didn't exist. "I feel terrible about not being with you yesterday." She reached out and covered his hand with hers. "I've never had such a miserable migraine in my life."

"It might have been brought on by the altitude," Mary offered, not caring whether she existed for Lee Stanton or not. "Being at nearly ten thousand feet affects some people that way."

Once again, Lee peered at Mary, her bright green eyes, narrow and cold. Since it had been dark when Lee arrived, this was Mary's first chance to really look at her. She was quite striking, even more so than Mary remembered. Her face was sharply sculptured, her lips full to the point of being exotic, her nose, slender, nostrils delicate.

Her skin was clear, pale, almost bloodless, as though she were allergic to sunshine. Her platinum hair was thick, the style, very short. It fell just shy of the length of her ears, leaving enough lobe visible to show off two-carat, diamond stud earrings. Her bangs, a narrow, platinum ribbon, bisected her forehead.

Every element of Lee Stanton, from her swan-like neck and svelte, nearly six-foot-tall form, her manicured nails to her Botox-injected forehead, spoke of practiced chic and the pursuit of physical perfection. Her white silk slacks and cowl-neck sweater screamed relaxed elegance. Mary sensed this woman didn't own a pair of jeans.

The stubby, Prince Valiant haircut seemed wildly paradoxical on Lee, who was the antithesis of unsophisticated and boyish. Her "innocent youth" coiffure bordered on fraud. At least that was Mary's opinion. Sadly, she wasn't objective on the subject of Bonner Wittering's girlfriend, no matter how badly she wanted to be.

"Well, aren't you a little fountainhead of information," Lee said to Mary. Her tone suggested she'd be perfectly content if Mary-the-fountainhead dried up and blew away. "Tell me, Marty, do you get a headache when you climb down out of the mountains?" She canted her head, her smile conniving. "Or do you know?"

"My name is Mary," she corrected, well aware Lee was calling her a country bumpkin whose opinion she found worthless, but she held her temper. "You shouldn't have a problem when you leave," she added. "If that's what you're asking."

"When will that be?" Pauline chimed in, as she served Bonn his breakfast. "Soon? I'll be happy to pack you a lunch for the drive."

Mary passed Pauline a quelling look, but the cook just smiled and shrugged.

"Thanks for the breakfast," Bonn said. "It looks delicious." Mary thought she heard the slightest tinge of mirth in his words, and found herself glancing his way. Their eyes met, but almost immediately he shifted his attention to Lee. "To answer your question, Pauline, I believe Lee told me she's staying until Wednesday." His lips twitched in a minimal grin. Mary couldn't tell if his mild amusement had been caused by the cook's smart-aleck remark or Lee's country bumpkin slam. "Speaking of leaving," he went on, "I talked to Miz Witty before I came down for breakfast, and she suggested a picnic this afternoon."

"Oh, how marvelous." Lee squeezed his hand. "I'd love it! How sweet of your old granny to think of me. And I haven't even had the pleasure of meeting her, yet."

"She wants to meet you." Bonn removed his hand from hers to pick up the syrup dispenser and drizzle the stuff over his waffles. "I'll introduce you after breakfast."

"Did you tell her who I *am?*" Lee asked. Mary wondered at the woman's tone. It seemed to be full of innuendo, but Mary couldn't imagine why.

Bonn set the pitcher down, picked up his knife and fork, then glanced at Lee briefly as he cut a bite of waffle. "I told her we're friends."

Since the mention of the picnic, Mary had tried to get her mind on something else, but she wasn't succeeding. She didn't mind Bonn and his ladylove going on a picnic. In fact, she was glad they were going. It would keep them *both* out from under foot. So why did she feel like she'd just eaten a bowl of concrete instead of oatmeal?

"Where'd you two meet, anyway?" Pauline asked as she poured herself a cup of coffee.

"Oh, we met at work," Lee said. "We're both—"

"*My* attorney and Lee are partners in the same law firm," Bonn cut in, his tone unusually sharp.

"Right," Lee said, with a laugh. "Bonn's in the office—a lot."

Mary's mind wrapped itself around what Bonn had just said. "*My attorney and Lee are partners in the same law firm.*" She became even more baffled. How did that answer fit into the high-fashion model business? She glanced at Bonn. "But isn't she a…" Mary hesitated, blinking as her brain belligerently confronted the truth. If Lee Stanton was a partner in a law firm, then she wasn't a high-fashion model. "But that would make her a…" She couldn't finish. The thought was too inconceivable.

Bonn met her gaze, finishing her sentence for her. "An attorney."

Hearing him say it didn't make it any more palatable. Mary's glance shot to Lee, and she echoed, "An attorney?" *Goodness!* Lee was gorgeous *and* a high-powered lawyer? Then she wasn't simply a tall, willowy, brainless beauty. She had a college degree, plus a law degree and was a partner in an important Boston law firm, which must mean she was exceptionally bright. She made tons of money, too. That was plain by her clothes and those rocks in her ears. Mary felt nauseous, old Trailer Town insecurities settling over her like a shroud. So—so maybe this beautiful, snippy blonde had a right to feel superior. She was.

Bonn's ironic chuckle drew her gaze. "Try to curb your enthusiasm, Miss O'Mara."

"What enthusiasm?" Lee asked, with a curt, sarcastic laugh. "She looks like somebody punched her in the stomach."

Mary reluctantly met his gaze; his earthy eyes held hers captive. "Mary thinks criminal defense attorneys are a waste of oxygen," he said, his grin crooked and cynical. Her heart raced ridiculously at the sight.

"Not all," Mary corrected, shifting her glance to Lee. "Just high-priced, smooth-talking lawyers whose sole business it is to prove that black is white or white is black, according to who's paying their fee!"

Lee burst out laughing. "Ouch. If looks could kill, I'd be dead!" She leaned forward aggressively, eyeing Mary. "One day, when you get into really bad trouble, sweet-cheeks, it's somebody exactly like me you'll run to. Trust me, you'll revisit your holier-than-thou attitude."

"That's enough, Lee," Bonn cautioned.

Lee glanced at him, then grinned sweetly. "Sure, baby. Whatever you say." Her gaze drifted back to Mary, her expression mutating to a cool smirk.

Lee's superior attitude didn't surprise Mary. She knew Lee didn't give a fig for her or her opinion. Without a doubt, one of the reasons Lee excelled in an adversarial career like criminal law was her invulnerability to the pain she caused others.

"I didn't think a client and his lawyer could have—a thing," Pauline said, from her lounging position beside the coffeepot. "Aren't there, like, rules?"

"The legal profession has lots of rules," Bonn said.

Lee held up her mug and faced Pauline. "You might as well refill me, cookie, since coffee's all I'm having. And, as for the rules, I don't represent Bonn. His lawyer is Taggart Lancaster." She paused and passed an odd smile to Bonn, before adding, "Taggart is the only lawyer besides myself, in that firm, with any real—*talent*."

Bonn looked annoyed, which didn't make sense. Why should Lee's admission that Bonn's lawyer had talent annoy Bonn? She was about to ask when he sat back, his attention shifting from Lee to Mary. "By the way," he said, "Miz Witty wants you to join us on the picnic. She thinks you've been working too hard and need a break." He watched dispassionately as Mary absorbed his comment.

When his meaning hit, it hit hard, and the question on the tip of her tongue was swept away in her horror. *Miz Witty insists I go along with Bonn and Lee on a picnic—an utterly unwelcome third wheel?* What had her employer been thinking? It was out of the question. She opened her mouth to refuse, but before she could speak, Bonn cut in. "Naturally, I accepted for you." Pushing up from the table, he held a hand toward Lee. "Shall we go meet Miz Witty?"

The couple left before Mary could form words. She sat motionless, stewing. This was horrible! She didn't want to be around them, let alone be foisted off on them like a bothersome baby sister! Or worse, a chaperone! She groaned, covering her face with her hands. "Oh, Pauline! How can I get out of it?" she cried. "They don't want me along any more than they want food poisoning!"

She heard the scrape of wood against wood and realized Pauline was taking the chair Lee had occupied. Forlorn, she peeked out from between her hands to see the cook set down her coffee mug and grin. "If you figure a way out of going, I'll be happy to send a case of food poisoning in your place."

She giggled wickedly and rubbed her hands together. "I can set a little of my homemade mayonnaise in the windowsill, so it'll go bad in the sunshine. Then I'll run to the store for vanilla yogurt and strawberries. Just before they leave for the picnic, I stir the spoiled mayo in the yogurt, pack it in the basket, and presto! One sick blonde lawyer!'' She nodded, encouragingly. ''Good, huh?''

Mary pushed away her congealing oatmeal. ''It's very—er—scary of you to offer, but—no.'' She sighed long and low. ''What am I going to do?''

''You're gonna go.''

Mary shook her head. ''That's not an option, even if I wanted to go—*which I do not!* They don't want me along.''

''But Miz Witty does.'' Pauline quirked another impish grin. ''And Miss Migraine *doesn't.* I can't think of two better reasons to go.''

''Bonn doesn't,'' she murmured, recalling his impassive features as he watched her absorb the news.

Pauline lifted her mug and held it in both fists, her expression going contemplative. ''To tell the truth, I got the feeling he did.'' She peered at Mary, her brow knitting inquiringly. ''Didn't you?''

Mary experienced a prickle of exhilaration, wishing that were true. *No! No! No!* she admonished inwardly, working to quell the tingling rush. *You don't want that to be true, you foolish, foolish woman!*

But what if Pauline were right?

Worrying her lower lip, she stared at the cook, pondering her query. Well, she wasn't so much pondering as attempting to rescue bits and pieces of her wits from the whirlwind of useless gray matter spinning inside her skull. Finally, drained from the effort, she shook her head. She had to face facts. The idea that Bonn wanted her along on the picnic was tempting—to the weak-willed fool in her—but in reality the notion was absurd. *And rightly so!* She pushed up from the table. "No—that's crazy. I—I'll make some excuse."

Taggart watched Mary trek up the woodland pathway ten feet ahead. Lee trudged beside him, clinging to his arm, breathing heavily. She'd had to borrow a pair of his hiking boots, which, with two pairs of thick socks, almost fit. She'd also had to borrow—kicking and screaming all the way—a pair of Mary's jeans.

Mary was at least five inches shorter than Lee, so the jeans were comically short and, according to Lee, "baggy as a clown suit." She wore a red, cotton knit sweater, her own, and the only thing she'd packed in those two suitcases, casual enough for the hike up to the meadow. Taggart wasn't sure she'd make it, if her labored breathing was any indicator.

"How—much—farther?" she asked between gasps.

"About a quarter of a mile," he said, experiencing a spark of wry amusement at Lee's struggle. How could that be? How could he find anything funny? Mary was clearly as unhappy as he was, having been forced to come along. He didn't know what Miz Witty had said to her, but whatever it was, she'd obeyed, though with conspicuous reluctance.

She had insisted on carrying the picnic basket, which was probably a good thing, since Taggart had his hands full with Lee. She was a tall woman, and though she was very slender, she was not exactly a feather.

"A—quarter—of—a—mile!" Lee wheezed.

"I thought you were so delighted about going on a picnic."

"I was—when I thought it—included—driving to a nice little park—in town."

"A park in town?" he asked, incredulous. "In the Rocky Mountains you think people drive into town to picnic in a park?"

"Well—whatever I thought—it didn't include—a third party!"

"Lee," he cautioned under his breath, even though Mary was moving farther and farther ahead and couldn't hear their conversation.

"Or…" she went on, "…dressing like—a homeless person!"

"You look fine." His attention was focused on Mary's backside as she hiked up the slope. As she walked, her hips swayed enticingly, they were impossible to look away from.

Lee lifted an arm up to his shoulder, gripping hard. "Thank you—baby." Her softened tone and the close proximity of her voice to his ear told him she'd turned toward him. He made himself glance her way and received a wide smile for his trouble. "You always—know the—right thing to say."

He had no idea what he'd said, but let it go. "Thanks."

"Why don't—you let me—ride you piggy-back?" she asked, giving him her sexiest pout.

"Because I don't want to die of a heart attack."

She poked her lower lip out farther, apparently under the misguided impression that acting like a spoiled two-year-old would turn him to mush. "For a woman—of my height—I'm *not* heavy."

"We're almost there," he said. "Besides, I thought you spent an hour at the gym every morning on the stationary bike."

"But—there's air—in Boston!"

Any other time he would have found her agony amusing. He wished he could muster a lighter mood and enjoy her bellyaching, since she found everybody else's suffering amusing. "Quit whining, Stanton." He indicated Mary, charging forward, now at least thirty feet ahead. "She's carrying twenty pounds of food in that basket. Do you see her complaining?"

Lee gave the brunette an annoyed, squinty look. "I wish I didn't see her at all." She laced her fingers though his supporting hand at her waist. "Why on earth—did you *naturally* insist—she come along?"

He watched Mary, taking in her unconscious, sexy wiggle, her surefooted trek along the steep, rocky path, the buoyant sway of her long hair. Lord, she was beautiful, and kind and strong and vulnerable and caring—everything he'd thought he would never find again, after Annalisa's death. "Because..." A melancholy smile tugged at his lips. "I love her."

CHAPTER TEN

"YOU—*what?*" Lee hauled Taggart to a stop.

He pursed his lips, staring after Mary as she moved farther away. He was surprised at how effortlessly he'd said those words. As though his love for Mary were as much a part of him as his eyes or his heart. After Annalisa's death, he'd never thought he would be able to utter them again.

He inhaled the light scent of vanilla. The clearing must be nearer than he'd realized. "You heard me." Unwillingly, he shifted his attention from Mary to his ex-lover's shocked face.

She made a sound, like a grunt or a curt, disbelieving laugh. "Come now, baby!" She indicated Mary with a dismissive wave. "Her? That ignorant nursemaid?" She shook her head and rolled her eyes. "That's not even funny, Tag!"

He removed his supporting arm from around her waist. "I know it's not funny," he said, stonily. "It's hell. She thinks I'm Bonner Wittering, a man she despises," he ground out. "The only person she hates more than Bonner is his lawyer." His gut soured with the irony.

Lee planted her hands on her hips and stared at him, speculatively. "His lawyer?"

He dropped his gaze to the path, rocky and covered with pine needles. "Yeah."

He heard nothing but the shrill wind through the topmost bows of the evergreen forest. After a moment, a low-pitched laugh covered the sound of wind, and he shifted his attention to Lee's face. She was shaking her head, grinning. "Let me get this straight," she said, still chortling. "You love her, but she hates the man she thinks you are. And the only person she hates more than the man she thinks you are is—*you*." She watched him, her expression one of squinty amusement as she pinched his cheek. "You're wrong, baby. *That's hilarious!*"

He frowned at her with distaste. How typical of Lee to dismiss his desperate dilemma as trivial. "You really are a heartless witch, Lee."

"Am I, baby?" She took his arm in both of hers, looking more animated than deflated by his slight. "Or are you merely indulging in a little-boy pout because you couldn't coax the country wench into your bed, and you're taking it out on me?"

"That's nuts," he said. "I'm using Bonn's name, but I'm not Bonn."

"You're a *man*," she said, as though it were a bad thing. "If you ask me, this a temporary infatuation. You're rebounding from our breakup. It means nothing. In a month you'll see that and laugh.''

He glared in disbelief. ''I thought the person who got dumped did the rebounding, not the other way around.''

She shrugged, squeezing his captured arm to her breast. ''Well, it's obvious you're not thinking clearly,'' she said. ''Look at it logically, baby. You and the nursemaid have nothing in common. She's country, you're city. She's probably a school dropout. You're a Harvard educated attorney. She's poor white trash, and you're—''

''Cut it out,'' he growled. ''The way I feel about Mary isn't prosecutorial evidence you can discredit. Love doesn't care about differences. I don't care if she can't write her own name. I love her.''

He still marveled at the sound of it, stated aloud. Since the moment he'd met Mary he'd tried to kill his attraction to her. He hadn't wanted or needed another love in his life, had been content with the memory of his beloved Annalisa. But the attraction wouldn't die. It thrived even while being scorned and trampled, taking on a life all its own, swelling and sweetening until he could no longer hide from it.

He'd spent innumerable hours in solitude with Annalisa's memory these past few days, remem-

bering her, how she'd died the way she lived—
saving children. She had been a wonderful, un-
selfish woman. She wouldn't have wanted him to
suffer, to grieve all the rest of his life, alone.

Somewhere in the dead of night, mere hours
ago, this insight had liberated him from his prison
of denial. He let himself understand that he'd
fallen deeply in love with Mary O'Mara. The
feeling was so pure and right he could no longer
feel guilt. What's more he knew Annalisa would
be sad if he did.

Yet, finally admitting that he loved Mary,
forced him to face the larger tragedy. The sad,
ironic fact was, Mary could never know.

As an impostor, he could never tell her who he
was, never touch her or show her how he felt.
Because of his lie, he must live out his life, alone,
after all, burdened by the knowledge that he'd
found—yet could never have—something pure
and fine that might have been.

Restless, seeking some kind of solace no matter
how small, he cast his gaze about the forest, wishing the beauty and peace of this mountainside
woodland could take away his brooding hurt.

He searched for anything to lift his spirits and
spied a big-horned elk off in the distance.
Handsome, regal, its majestically ornamented
head held high, it stood still, seeming to sense

their presence. An instant later it bolted gracefully away, without a sound, through the dense pines.

Despite being favored with such a magnificent vision, Taggart's emptiness couldn't be filled, couldn't even be touched. ''I'm sure you'll find this funny, too,'' he went on grimly. ''Because of this charade, I can never tell her how I feel. I know that.''

''At least you're thinking logically on that point.'' Lee lifted his arm and lay it across her shoulders, trapping it there by lacing her fingers through his. She slid her other arm about his waist, holding on possessively. ''Let's go picnic. I feel a lot better.''

With Lee attached to him like a tick, Taggart trudged forward. ''However she feels about me,'' he said, ''it doesn't change the fact that I'm not in love with you.''

''Hush.'' She squeezed his waist. ''We have plenty of time to talk about who loves whom, and what constitutes a successful marriage partnership, once we're back in Boston.''

Taggart didn't respond. He wasn't in the mood for a debate, and he knew Lee too well to believe she would concede a point before both sides spilled blood. She could believe whatever she wanted, it wouldn't change anything. Sooner or later she would have to face the fact that their relationship—at least their sexual one—was over.

Beyond the trees the path ended in the brightly lit meadow. A few more steps and Taggart could see the brook, sparkling in the sun. A half dozen more paces along the steep, rugged path, and he could hear it babble as it rushed over its shallow, rocky bed. Not far away, on the other side of the frolicking water, Mary spread the picnic blanket amid a vast mantle of flowers that gave a bluish-violet cast to the meadowland.

"Well, there's Matilda, getting everything ready." Even without looking at Lee, Taggart sensed her self-satisfied grin. "Maybe it was better, after all," she went on, "having a serving girl along to fetch and carry and set the table."

"Stanton," he muttered, "you call her anything but Mary, ever again, and I'll toss you off a cliff."

She laughed outright. "Ooooh, I love it when you get macho, Tag."

"And you call me anything but Bonn, and I'll—"

"Stop it! Stop it!" she cried, sounding both gleeful and taunting. "One more manly command, and I'll be forced to jump you in front of God and—*Mary*—and all the stupid, furry beasts up here that haven't perished from oxygen deprivation!"

* * *

Mary tried to ignore the entwined couple as they entered the clearing, strove to overlook the carnal note in Lee's laughter. She felt like an invisible lackey, brought along to bow and scrape for the lord and his lady.

Sucking in a deep breath to quell her embarrassment, she began to lay out the food Pauline had prepared. It looked good—fried chicken, potato salad, chewy, home-baked bread doused with seasoned butter, tangy lemonade and chocolate-chocolate-chip cupcakes. Mary knew Pauline's picnic lunches were the best in the world, but her stomach churned so badly she didn't think she could eat a bite.

"Hi, hi," Lee sang out with a broad wave and a toothy grin. Mary wondered at her lightened spirits. The pretty lady lawyer had begun the trek looking as glum as any big-city socialite in somebody else's ill-fitting jeans and too large hiking boots could look. Apparently something along the way had caused her attitude to improve. Mary didn't want to dwell on what that something might have been. The couple had lagged so far behind they could have...

She ruthlessly shut out the sexy image that flashed in her mind. Thinking about it could only make her more upset.

"Aren't you sweet to get everything ready," Lee cooed, slithering languidly from Bonn's arms to seat herself on the blanket. "Whew, I don't know how you mountain folk stand this thin air," she went on gaily. "You must be half mountain goat."

Mary didn't think Lee meant that goat remark as a compliment, but she maintained her poise. "If you two don't mind, I think I'll go back to the house. I have a headache—"

"Don't be silly." Lee lifted a hand toward Mary as though expecting her to take it. Well, she'd have an excruciating wait before *that* happened. "Sit. Join us." Seeming to comprehend Mary's loathing to accept her hand, Lee dropped it and patted the blanket. "I won't hear of you carrying that heavy basket all the way up here and not eating any of this delightful food."

That statement surprised Mary. She didn't think Lee would have a good word to say about such a fatty lunch. Pauline had joked privately that she hoped "Miss Skinny Snob" wouldn't be able to find anything she could eat, and be forced to forage for berries and drink from the brook. Mary had a feeling Lee wouldn't be the one foraging or toting water, she would, but she hadn't commented.

"Please, Mary," Bonn said, quietly. "Stay." His expression was so serious she almost believed he meant it. He was good, she had to give him that—with that ability to look sincere. Of course, it was possible he did mean it, since he was trying desperately to keep Miz Witty from changing her will. He knew winning over Mary could only benefit him and his sleazy scheme. That was all the more reason to leave.

Except, Miz Witty has specifically asked that Mary go along on the picnic. She hadn't said why, hadn't insisted she go. She'd simply taken Mary's hands in hers, and very solemnly, her eyes beseeching, had said, ''Please, Mary. Do this for me.''

Remembering the glimmer of emotion in Miz Witty's eyes and her earnest, imploring expression, Mary reluctantly took a seat on the wool, plaid blanket. ''Okay. For a while,'' she murmured, not making any effort to hide her aversion. She shifted her gaze from Bonn to Lee. The woman's strange smile caused a tremor of apprehension to creep down her spine.

''Excellent!'' Lee's attention slid to the dishes laid out before her. ''We can get to know one another.''

Mary couldn't think of anything she'd rather not do, but kept that to herself.

''Sit, sit,'' Lee said to Bonn. ''You'll give Mary and me stiff necks standing there like some Civil War statue.''

Mary tried not to look at Bonn as he took a seat across from her. ''Plates, napkins and flat-

ware are in the basket.'' She concentrated on un-
covering the dishes. ''Bonn, please pass them
out.''

Twenty minutes later, Mary had forced down
all she could stomach, which had been a single
chicken leg, a teaspoon of potato salad and two
gulps of lemonade. She noticed that Lee had eaten
about as much. Bonn had been the only one to
actually consume enough food to be considered a
meal.

Mary stayed out of the conversation unless spoken to directly. She responded in mumbled mono-
syllables, making it so hard for the couple to draw
her into the dialogue, they finally left her out al-
together. Which was fine with her. She just
wanted this hideous disaster *over*.

''What are you looking at, Bonn?'' Lee asked,
drawing Mary's unwilling attention to the man
across from her.

He peered off in the distance, toward the far
edge of the meadow before it dropped off into a
canyon. The sun on his face highlighted the sharp
beauty of his features and gave his earthy eyes an
added golden glint that was terribly unfair.
''Grazing elk,'' he said, resting that breathtaking,
gilded glance briefly on Mary before he faced
Lee.

Even though his gaze had hardly been more
than a glancing blow, Mary sizzled with its effect.

She cursed herself inwardly and fought the feeling, her emotions fraying and tattering. She wondered how much longer she could combat her attraction to him before she reached the point of utter emotional exhaustion?

And then what?

"Elk? Really?" Lee craned her long, pale neck in that direction. "If you want a closer look, don't mind us. We'll be here when you get back."

He gave her a narrowed look, as though gauging her motives. "It's no big deal."

Lee waved away his refusal. "Go on. Go look at the big, bad elk." She smiled at him. "I never realized you were such a mammalogist."

He watched her for another moment, one eyebrow lifting in question. "Mammalogist?" he repeated, sounding dubious. "Is that the scientific term for a Textbook Playboy?"

She laughed, the sound powerful and hearty, almost masculine. "No, baby, that would be Mammary *Gland*-alogist."

Mary scanned Bonn's face as he stared at Lee. He didn't react to her suggestive pun.

Lee made shooing motions. "Go on." She picked up a cupcake and thrust it at him. "Spy on the wildlife. We'll be fine."

"You'll play nice, right?" he said.

Lee reached out and pinched his cheek. "I promise, baby."

Mary couldn't understand what Bonn might mean by his question about playing nice. What did he think would happen, that his girlfriend would belittle her? Was he worried Lee might mess up his ploy to get on Mary's good side? She eyed him with her most hostile expression. "If you're afraid she'll tell me your faults, don't panic. My low opinion of you is set in concrete. Nothing Lee might add could damage it further."

He deposited the cupcake with the others, his concerned gaze shifting to Mary. "Thanks for your reassurance." His jaw muscles knotted. "So," he added, his eyes still on her, "if you'll excuse me?"

Hadn't she made it crystal clear she didn't want him around? The breeze danced with her hair and she pushed it out of her eyes. "Personally, I can hardly wait." Breaking eye contact, she picked up her lemonade glass and took a swig. Inwardly she cried, *Don't come back. Please! You're making me crazy, trying to hate you, trying not to care that you and Lee are lovers, trying to forget how devastating your kisses are and how foolishly I crave them! Yes, go! Get out of my sight—and my heart!*

Bonn stood and walked toward the edge of the wood. Mary ignored him with all her strength. Luckily he had to go behind her to approach the elk so she was freed from her battle to keep from looking at him.

"Well," Lee said, leaning back on her hands. "Alone at last."

Mary glanced at the blonde, disconcerted by her antagonistic tone. The smile Lee had worn so effusively during the picnic lunch was gone. "You have a crush on him, don't you?"

Mary frowned, mystified. "I beg your pardon?"

"Don't be dense." Lee wagged a hand in Bonn's direction. "Bonner Wittering. You're nuts about him."

Mary's cheeks heated. She was shocked by the blunt statement, and unsettled that her involuntary reaction had been so—so guilty. She was momentarily speechless. When she found her voice, it was weak, stuttery. "Why—why, *no!*" She battled to gather her composure. "I work for his grandmother. I love her and I don't want to see her hurt." She swallowed, formulating in her mind what she wished were true, but knowing it was a lie. "My feelings for Mr. Wittering depend totally on how he treats his grandmother."

Lee's expression remained severe, skeptical. After a minute, she smiled, but the twist of her lips was more calculating than friendly. "Oh, nursey, if I had you on the witness stand, I'd tear that fairy story to shreds in thirty seconds."

Mary stiffened, upset and angry at being called a liar. The fact that she *had* lied only made her resentment harder to conceal. "What are you trying to say, Miss Stanton?"

Lee looked in the direction Bonn had gone. "Nothing. Except don't set your sights too high, country girl." She lounged back on an elbow, looking relaxed in her haughty superiority. "I know how a person like you must feel when a man like Bonn comes along. You start to think, 'Here's my ticket out of this stale life as an old lady's nursemaid.'" Lee tilted her head, the image of sly self-satisfaction. "I can understand how you feel. It's normal to want to better yourself. But as far as Ta—er—Bonner Wittering is concerned, it's not going to happen. You see, Bonn and I are…" She paused, her expression smug. "Well, let's just say, he's *taken,* and let it go at that." She patted Mary's knee, the act reeking with condescension. "I'm sure one day you'll find some beefy lumberjack, and you'll both be happy raising your brood of baby lumberjacks up here on your mountain." She squeezed Mary's knee. "You and Bonn are simply not in the same league. No offense, but facts are facts."

Mary stared at Lee, so glib and insolent. Clearly this woman had never had a moment's doubt about what *league* she played in. She knew nothing of how it felt to grow up in Trailer Town or what poverty was like, wearing donated cast-offs from taunting classmates, or eating rice and beans three times a day, because by the end of the month, money and groceries were gone, and there was nothing else left.

Just because Lee Stanton had been born into wealth and privilege, she didn't have a right to be condescending and snide. She didn't have the right to make assumptions about who Mary might fall in love with, or suggest her motives were self-ish. "First, Miss Stanton," she said quietly, "Get your hand off my knee." Lee's smarmy smile vanished. She lifted her hand away as though it had been burned.

Mary brushed her hair back with both hands. "Second, I wouldn't have Bonner Wittering if he were covered with cream cheese icing and had 'Take me!' printed across his chest. I find him detestable." She tried to mean it with her whole, wayward heart. "Whatever gave you the insane idea I felt anything but disgust for him?"

"Why, he told me, naturally." Lee sat up and crossed her arms. "On the way up the trail. He told me how crazy you are about him. How embarrassingly obvious it is." She eyed Mary with a contemptuous sneer. "He thinks you're terribly funny. I was just trying to help you, dear." A well-shaped brow rose, the pause pregnant. "You know, girl to girl. You seem like a nice kid. I don't want to see you get hurt.''

Sure, not unless you can do it yourself! Mary felt sick. How could he possibly know? She must not be as good at hiding her stubborn infatuation as she'd thought she was. She'd done nothing but fling insults at him. Was he so adept at reading women that he'd seen through her? Had it been her eyes that betrayed her? Or was it her foolish kiss on the front porch?

She swallowed hard. This was awful, horrible, the worst humiliation she could imagine. Bonn, with his insidious genius to appear sincere and sympathetic, had been laughing at her behind her back the whole time!

Mary forced her jumbled, wounded emotions into some semblance of order. Though weak in the knees, she pushed herself up to stand. Her posture stiff and proud, she said, ''I appreciate your—concern, Lee. But—it's unnecessary. I detest Mr. Wittering more than any human being on earth.'' She stepped off the blanket and headed down the slope toward the brook. ''Feel free to quote me!''

CHAPTER ELEVEN

TAGGART awoke Tuesday, July twenty-ninth, to the news that it was Founder's Day in Wittering, Colorado. According to Ruby and Pauline, the only people in the kitchen when he had come down to breakfast, Founder's Day was a local holiday, complete with a carnival, topped off by a dance in the town hall that night. He didn't recall hearing a word about it until now, but he'd been too blasted preoccupied, especially since the picnic, to know much of anything that didn't involve Mary.

When he'd come back to the high country meadow after fifteen minutes of watching the family of elk, Lee sat alone, a Cheshire cat grin on her face. She'd insisted—on her honor as an officer of the court—that she hadn't said anything to Mary about his confession of love, hadn't called her "Myrtle" or made any insulting remarks. Lee insisted Mary had simply said she had work to do and hurried off.

Taggart wasn't stupid. He knew something had happened, and berated himself for leaving the two of them alone. The minute he'd gotten out of earshot he'd felt in his gut it wasn't a bright thing to do. Why hadn't he gone with his instincts? Why did he continue to trust Lee? She was devious, and heaven only knew what trouble she might concoct, just for fun.

The next time Taggart saw Mary, the antagonism in her eyes scalded the very air in his lungs. If he'd thought she'd hated him before, he'd been a naive idiot. She detested him now with a laser-hot passion. Every time he chanced to gaze into those smoky eyes, the incendiary flare scorched him to the depths of his being.

His heart was charred, his soul gutted, because that's what the absence of hope did to a man. He had no choice but to hide his pain. He'd made a promise to Bonner that had to be kept, no matter how bitterly he suffered. He liked Miz Witty, and the last thing on earth he planned to do was break her heart.

The eldery Mrs. Wittering was the one bright spot for Taggart on this balmy Founder's Day. Since Mary had the afternoon off to spend with her half sister, Becca, Taggart volunteered to wheel Bonner's grandmother through the carnival booths and rides. She was full of fun, and plainly relished every minute she spent with the man she believed to be her grandson. Her joy even managed to elevate Taggart's dour mood somewhat.

On the other hand, Lee's possessive presence wore at him, threatening to drag his mood back down. Taggart's law partner was at her most charming in front of Miz Witty, but he knew she would love to lock the elderly Mrs. Wittering in a closet rather than spend a minute with her, let alone a whole afternoon. Although Miz Witty was equally cheerful and appeared to be delighted with the threesome, Taggart sensed that deep down, she disliked the blond lawyer from Boston.

Consequently, they were a trio of actors on the Wittering town stage, showing little, if any, of their true feelings. The outing would have been an excruciating sham, except for the unexpected satisfaction he felt every time Miz Witty looked at him with tenderness and love in her eyes. Though he knew she thought he was somebody else, he relished her grandmotherly affection. Except for his wife, Annalisa, in his whole life, Taggart could hardly recall seeing expressions of unconditional love from anyone. He'd never known his own grandparents, and he'd been so young when his parents died.

He was stunned to realize that in just over a week he'd become quite attached to Bonner's grandmother. He was amazed at how much like family he felt toward her. She was a bright, optimistic person with a generous nature and a kind heart. She deserved to be happy, to be cherished by her only living relative, not abandoned by him.

Taggart could tell he wasn't the only person who felt that way about her, by the enthusiastic way townsfolk greeted her. She was unquestionably a much loved and revered woman. He despised himself for deceiving her. Yet, how much more would she be hurt if she knew the truth? How much of a jolt could her heart stand? No. Telling her the truth was a chance he didn't dare take.

Taggart heard a familiar voice and turned to see Pauline smiling at him from inside the kissing booth. She waved. "Come on over, Mr. Wittering," she said. "It's all for a good cause." She was dressed in the usual plaid shirt and jeans, the buttons all doing their job.

She indicated Jed, standing alongside the booth, his expression quietly pleased. "Don't worry, my sweetie here will keep everything on the up-and-up." She reached out and affectionately touched Jed's arm. "One kiss, one dollar. No hands or tongues. Help buy new computers for Wittering Middle School."

"Go on, Bonny," Miz Witty said, reaching back and caressing his hand, resting on the chair handle. "Then we can wheel over to the *other* kissing booth for Lee and me."

"Other kissing booth?" Taggart asked, with a questioning grin.

Miz Witty wagged her brows, impishly. "Yes, *other!* I know it's been a long time since you've been here, but Wittering's become very progressive. For the last five Founder's Days we've had a kissing booth for the women, too."

"Well, that is progressive," Taggart said with a chuckle. He wheeled Miz Witty to Pauline's booth and fished a five dollar bill from his wallet. "Here you go," he said.

Pauline took it, looked at it and grinned. "Five kisses, it is." She placed the bill in a metal box on the counter and presented Taggart with puckered lips.

He leaned over the booth's partition, kissed her cheek, then stepped back to grin at her. "It's intimidating kissing a woman in front of her boyfriend." He indicated the mechanic. "He's pretty big."

Jed smiled shyly but didn't speak.

Pauline guffawed. "You got a point." She jerked a thumb toward Lee. "Your lady lawyer ain't no stringbean, either."

Taggart chuckled, experiencing a surge of true amusement for the first time since the picnic. His sideways glance at Lee told him she hadn't found the exchange particularly entertaining. Indicating the lawyer, he said, "She's tall, but she hardly weighs a thing." He winked at Pauline. "She told me so herself."

"Hilarious," Lee said through thinned lips. "Where's that other kissing booth?" She directed her question at Jed, who averted his eyes, indicating the location with the jerk of his chin. "Thanks," Lee said, sounding sarcastic. "Word to the wise, fella—don't chatter so much." She took Taggart's arm as he wheeled Miz Witty away through the milling, laughing throng. "When can we dump the old lady and be alone?" she whispered.

Taggart gave her a look that didn't bode well for her fantasy life. "When she wants to go home, we go."

"Oh, pleeeease," she moaned in his ear.

"Stanton," he muttered, under his breath, "nobody forced you to come."

"Why there's Mary and Becca," Miz Witty said, waving. "Mary!" she called. "Mary O'Mara!"

Taggart spotted her beyond the throng. She and a waif of a little girl with long, straight blond hair sat on a bench at the trolley stop. They were across the street from the supermarket parking lot serving as the carnival grounds. The town's main thoroughfare had been blocked off to automobile traffic for the Founder's Day celebration.

Becca sat in Mary's lap, her thin arms curled about her big sister's neck. The child's face was animated. She smiled broadly as she talked. Mary held her, looking sweetly maternal, stroking her little sister's hair.

Too many people ambled about, laughing and chitchatting. Too much noise rang through the air, with hawkers calling folks to their booths and the loud, tinny music piped from the towering Ferris wheel. A nearby merry-go-round spun, filled with children shrieking with laughter. Colored lights flashed in time to its tooting tune, drowning out any hope that Miz Witty's greeting could be heard.

"Oh, let's not bother them," Miz Witty said, to Taggart. Her tone suggested she was touched by the heartwarming sight. "Let's leave them alone. Mary and Becca get so little time together, and they look so happy."

"Excellent idea." Lee tugged on Taggart's elbow. "Let's find the beer tent."

"Oh, dear me, no," Miz Witty said to Lee. "I don't believe in imbibing." She pointed off in another direction, beyond the merry-go-round. "There's Joshua Hanna, our best-looking local hunk, manning the women's kissing booth. He's such a dear. Let's go give to charity until it hurts."

"Well, well," Lee said, apparently pleased with what she saw. "I, for one, suddenly feel extremely civic-minded. I think I'll make a *large* donation, too."

As they moved off toward the local hunk, Taggart divided his attention between their destination and Mary. She laughed at something Becca said. Her features were beautiful in happy animation. Though he couldn't hear her, he imagined the light, tinkling sound, and experienced a gut punch of desire. She kissed her sister's forehead and smoothed her yellow sweater.

A man, appearing around fifty years old, came up behind them and said something that made them both jump and stare. The man was stocky, with a noticeable paunch. His squared-off features were shadowed by several days growth of gray beard, his salt-and-pepper hair unkempt. He wore a black T-shirt with a heavy metal band's name emblazoned in red across the front. A tattoo covered his left arm from wrist to elbow. He looked angry, shouted something and grasped Becca by the wrist.

Mary stood up, hiking the child on one hip, but the man didn't release the tiny wrist.

"Who's that with Mary and her sister?" Taggart asked, drawing Miz Witty's attention back to the bench.

"Oh, dear!" She sounded upset. "That's Joe Lukins, Becca's father."

The man pulled Becca bodily away from Mary, lifting her over the back of the bench. Becca burst into tears and Mary said something to the man, her body language making her anger clear. Joe Lukins made a brusque, dismissive gesture and turned away to stalk off. Mary rounded the bench, grasped his arm, but he dislodged her hold with a jerk.

"Oh, no," Miz Witty said. "That barbarian promised he'd let Becca stay at the carnival all afternoon." She looked at her wristwatch. "It's barely three!"

Taggart experienced a surge of outrage as Mary chased the rapidly retreating Joe. She exhibited her fury, shouting, curling her hands into fists of frustration. Becca sobbed, stretching her spindly arms back over her father's shoulder in a pleading gesture.

"That bastard." He released Miz Witty's chair, intent on stopping the jerk.

"Hold it there, Boy Scout." Lee clutched his arm. "Where do you think you're going?"

He gave her a hostile glare. "That bastard can't do that."

"Yes, that bastard can," she said, with a cautioning lift of an eyebrow. "If that's the kid's father, he can do whatever he wants. I'm a *law-*

yer," she said, her emphasis on the word a not-so-subtle warning. "We *lawyers* know these things."

He clenched his teeth, scowling at her, wishing she were wrong. A moment later he refocused on Mary and her troubles. By now, she'd stopped chasing Lukins, and Becca's thin arms no longer reached out. Her little fists covered her eyes and she cried helplessly.

The scene was difficult to watch and do nothing about. But Lee was right. His interference would do no good. Lukins had done nothing that was against any law. If Taggart butted in, the jerk would have every right to call the sheriff. Taggart couldn't afford that. Any involvement with law enforcement would expose his real identity. The trip was almost over, almost a success—at least as far as Miz Witty's happiness was concerned.

Lips thinned, nostrils flaring at being reduced to the status of powerless spectator, he glared at Lukins. The man appeared unmoved by his daughter's grief as he stalked to a pickup truck, its tailgate butted up to the temporary road barrier. He opened the passenger door and dumped the fragile child into the arms of a frowzy redhead.

"Who's the woman?" he asked.

"Joe's latest girlfriend, I suppose." Miz Witty shook her head. "Poor Becca. Poor Mary." She fisted her pale, blue-veined hands on the arms of her wheelchair. "That coldhearted brute doesn't deserve that child."

Joe slammed the passenger door, tramped around to the driver's side and jumped in. A minute later the truck disappeared down the street.

"Come on, Bonny," Miz Witty coaxed, touching his hand. "It's a sad situation, but there's nothing we can do. Joe's the child's father. I wish we could comfort Mary, but knowing her as I do, she'll want to be alone—so she can gather herself together. She's very private that way." Miz Witty's touch drew his attention but not his gaze. He continued to watch Mary.

She stood with her back to them, her long, shiny hair fluttering in the breeze. Her posture spoke of her dejection, her head down, one hand covering her mouth. Even from a distance of at least ten car lengths, Taggart swore he could detect her fingers trembling.

He ached to go to her, hold her, but he knew his attempt to comfort her would be as welcome as the sting of a scorpion.

Mary could hardly tolerate the idea of going to the Founder's Day dance. Her much anticipated afternoon with Becca had turned out so badly, ended so cruelly. She and Becca had spent little more than an hour together before Joe ruined everything by showing up, growling that Becca'd had enough "excitement" for one day, and dragged her off. What possible harm could it have done the five-year-old to spend two more measly hours at a carnival on a beautiful day, with her big sister?

They hadn't even begun to play games or go on rides. Having just finished lunch and thinking they had all the time in the world, they'd walked to the bench to visit and let the hot dogs and milkshakes settle. Then suddenly, *blam,* Becca was gone.

Again.

Mary had been surprised to see Joe with a vehicle, since he'd totaled his car last year. His license had been revoked for driving drunk. She feared he was driving without a license. Though she couldn't be sure, she was terrified that he'd begun drinking again. If that were true, the man was a ticking time bomb. A wave of alarm had swept through her. How dare he put Becca at such great risk! When she'd challenged him, he cursed at her and threatened that she mind her own business or she'd be sorry.

Mary was so emotionally devastated she would never have considered going to the dance, if it hadn't been for Miz Witty's insistence. She couldn't imagine working up enough strength to do anything but stay in her room and cry her heart out. On the other hand, Mary felt an obligation toward her employer. Founder's Day was a hugely important event for Miz Witty, especially since she was the only living descendant of the town's founder. Well, except for Bonner Wittering.

Her heart twisted at the thought of him. The insufferable egomaniac actually had the unmitigated gall to brag that *she* had a crush on him. And he'd bragged to—*of all people*—his equally insufferable lawyer-lover. Every time the thought reared its ugly head in her mind, she wanted to die. All this time, he'd been laughing at her!

It made her crazy. She wanted to scratch out his eyes and kick his shins until they were black and blue and—and—and…she swallowed hard, blinking back tears. She was relieved the rustic town hall was lit with nothing more than rope after rope of tiny, white holiday lights, strung in twisted strands along the walls and cobwebbed across the ceiling like stars. She wanted so badly to feel nothing for Bonner she'd found herself wishing for release from his insidious charisma on the fake stars strung overhead. It hadn't worked—but what did she expect from *fake* stars? Trying anything so bizarre only proved how far gone she was.

She'd wiped away too many tears since she'd arrived at the dance, over her ridiculous fixation for such an amoral man. *Thank heaven and the decorating committee for the dim lighting!*

A local Western band performed at the front of the auditorium. On the dance floor, couples shuffled cheek-to-cheek. Along the back of the room, a row of decorated tables trembled under the weight of delectable munchies contributed by the partygoers. A separate table held a huge bowl of sparkling punch and two urns of rich coffee. Metal folding chairs lined the side walls so Wittering citizens weary of dancing could relax and gossip.

Much to Mary's discomfort, the band had been playing more slow, romantic songs than rousing boot-stompin' tunes. Sadly, she supposed she wasn't dressed for boot-stomping, in three-inch heels and the gauzy, pink ankle-length dress she'd ordered from a catalog. The sleeveless, low cut style was too summery for high altitude evenings, that could be cold even in midsummer, so Miz Witty had insisted Mary borrow her exquisite pink, crocheted wrap, perfect for the dress and the chilly night air.

Mary had never attended Wittering's annual Founder's Day dance until she started working for Miz Witty. Trailer Town teens rarely went. It was no fun going to a party when you knew your best dress was a hand-me-down or garage sale purchase from one of the better-off women who would be there.

Working for Miz Witty, earning a living, made everything different. For the past two years, she'd enjoyed the dances. This year, however, she would have preferred to melt into the shadows. Her heart wasn't in the mood—with Bonner and Becca both tugging on her heartstrings. The only problem with remaining in the shadows was the scarcity of unattached females. Wittering was one of the rare places where men outnumbered women. So, for Miz Witty, Mary put on her party face and danced and laughed and tried with all her might not to seek out Bonner Wittering with her eyes, her mind or her heart.

It wasn't easy, since Lee fairly glittered. Her snowy, silk blouse had a trillion sparkly rhinestone buttons running down the front, with a dozen more strung along each wide cuff. Add the sparkle of those huge diamond rocks in her ears and, well, she practically caught fire with reflected light every time she moved. Her slim, black skirt fit like a sausage skin—one of those creations only mannequins and half-starved models could pull off, but Lee managed. She was so tall, so thin, so sophisticated, so educated. Every time Mary's glance fell on the lady lawyer, she felt a little more dowdy and puffy and boring.

The dance ended and Mary's partner, a local mail carrier, thanked her and escorted her to the fruit punch table. She'd used the "If you'll excuse me, I'd like to get something to drink" plea so many times tonight, she was beginning to fear going into sugar shock.

She smiled a mute "goodbye" to the gangly man and turned her attention to the paper punch cups. Nervous and out-of-sorts, she straightened several, turning them so the flower designs faced out. Another slow, seductive melody began. When she was sure her latest partner had moved off into the crowd, she took a step back from the table and slammed into someone. By the solidness of the body, she knew it was a man. A big man, she decided, since he hadn't stumbled backward when she'd rammed him. "Oh, excuse me, I should have looked where I—"

She turned to find herself staring into Bonner Wittering's dark eyes. Her apology and her polite smile died a quick death. Apparently, so did her brain, since she could do nothing but gawk.

"No problem, Miss O'Mara," he said softly. "I've been stepped on before." His lips quirked vaguely, as though he might smile. He didn't quite. She wondered why he bothered to hide his amusement from her, since he obviously found her easy to laugh at when her back was turned. "To be honest, you're not the first woman to step on me tonight.'' He held out a hand. ''I was about to ask you to dance.'' He indicated the dimly lit room, pulsating with entwined couples. ''You'd have complete freedom to stomp on me out there. I have a feeling you'd enjoy that.''

He wasn't wrong about her desire to stomp on him, but no matter how much she wanted to agree, she didn't respond, couldn't move. Before she realized what was happening, he took her hand and tugged her into his arms. An instant later, their bodies softly impacting, they swayed to the sultry melody.

Mary blinked, stared blankly into his white dress shirt. She didn't like to think it, but he looked gorgeous, in dark slacks, beige sports coat and pristine dress shirt open at the neck. He smelled delicious, too, manly, clean, with a hint of spicy aftershave. The kind of smell you wanted to bury your nose in and just breathe until you passed out.

She resisted the urge, holding her face away from his shirtfront. She couldn't help but notice that he held her like a real Western dance partner would hold a woman. Bellies rubbing, knees brushing. His hand rested gently, yet firmly, at the small of her back, his fingers spread, warm and unsettlingly welcome. He cupped her other hand against his heart. She could feel its slow, measured beat beneath her palm. He swayed with her to the music, so easy to follow, the sum of his parts an erotic whole that grew harder to resist with every strum of the guitar.

"You look lovely tonight," he whispered, drawing her gaze and dispersing the haze that had begun to cloud her brain.

He wasn't smiling, but watching her with that pseudo-sincerity that looked so disarmingly real. His eyes held a troubling allure. She threw up her guard, hardening her heart against the sensory onslaught. "I'd rather not talk, if you don't mind."

His brow creasing, he looked away for an instant before snagging her gaze again and nodding. "Of course."

They danced on. Though Mary concentrated on staring at his shirt, she felt his eyes on her hair, her face, her throat, her bare shoulder where the wrap had slipped. Time seemed to stop, but they danced on. Mary sighed deeply, wishing she could remain in his arms forever, wishing he weren't a cavalier playboy, a thoughtless, conniving snake. Wanting him to be just one of the Wittering men, an honest, average guy. Longing for the look in his eyes to be genuine. Despairing that he was not a man worthy of undying love.

"I'm sorry about what happened with Becca this afternoon," he said, startling her so badly she forgot her request that they not speak.

"How do you know about that?"

"We saw," he said, looking sympathetic. "Have you tried the courts—getting custody?"

She winced at the irony of his question. "Me?" She shook her head. "No, but Joe has."

"What?"

She shrugged. "Mom left a will stating she wanted me to have Becca part of the year. Joe didn't want that, so he took me to court. It ended with me getting Becca the first two weeks every August, for Becca's birthday, and every other Christmas." She felt tears welling and blinked them back. "And Joe can't change residences without letting me know first. When the judge upheld my mother's wishes, it made Joe furious and even more determined to keep us apart. He does his best to obstruct anything that's not strictly documented in the ruling. He cancels our plans at the last minute, or like today, Becca and I get together, but Joe shows up early and makes her leave before she's supposed to."

She wiped at a tear and looked away, embarrassed. "As mean-spirited as Joe is, he's her father. Courts don't take children away from their natural parents without good reason, and being a jerk isn't a good enough reason." She chanced a quick look at his face but those eyes were so powerful in their charismatic pull, she quickly looked away. "Friday's August first, so I get her for two whole weeks. Thank heaven he can't do anything to ruin that.''

Bonner didn't speak for a long time, long enough for Mary to have to fight the effects of his subtle attraction again. She was sorry she'd said she didn't want them to talk. At least dialogue got her mind on something beside how good he smelled, or how sexily he danced. She felt tingly all over, and hot. Her breathing came in forced, little gasps. ''Well?'' she asked, panicky, needing conversation, *any conversation,* even if it had to be the unhappy topic of Joe Lukins. If she didn't get her mind wrapped around something else very soon, she was afraid she'd rear up on her toes and kiss him again!

''Well, what?'' he asked, his breath caressing her cheek, a warm, seductive whisper that made her weak in the knees.

''Don't you have anything you want to say to me?'' she asked, her voice high-pitched.

His expression was unreadable, his dark eyes reflecting the tiny, white lights, but nothing more. His jaw hardened and a muscle jumped in his cheek. After a drawn-out moment, he shook his head, looking oddly regretful. ''No, Mary,'' he murmured, ''there's nothing I can say.''

CHAPTER TWELVE

TAGGART sat on the edge of his bed. Restless, he checked his watch. Nearly eight o'clock. Lee would be finishing breakfast. In a few minutes she needed to leave, to drive to the Denver airport for her noon flight back to Boston. He planned to go down to say goodbye, but didn't intend to spend one more moment with her than necessary.

These past six days with her dogging his heels, refusing to believe anything but her own deluded fantasies about the two of them wore him down. With the lie he was living on Bonner's behalf, and then so unexpectedly discovering Mary, who kept him tripping over his heart, he had precious little charity left for Lee's persistent pawing and clinging.

He slumped forward to rest his forearms on his thighs, recalling last night and the party in a log lodge, decorated so simply with hundreds of tiny, twinkling lights. Even the memory rejuvenated his weary soul and brought a smile to his face. The modest party, attended by ordinary towns-folk, seemed like it took place on a faraway planet. Wittering was so different from all he dealt with as a Boston trial lawyer—antagonistic courtroom environments, clashes with rival attorneys, hostile prosecutors, not to mention dealing with the fears and egos of wealthy, whiny clients.

He wished he didn't have to leave on Friday, wished he never had to leave. He wished he'd met Mary in a completely different way, maybe on a ski trip. Okay, so he was a lawyer. That didn't make him the devil incarnate. So he had clients who were more worm than human. It was the nature of the beast. Even worms deserved a strenuous defense. Sometimes he won when his gut told him he shouldn't have, but most of the time the system worked the way it was designed to.

Yeah, Taggart, but there are days when you'd chuck the whole thing! a less defensive part of his brain whispered. *Not only the hassles of defending clients who had more money than morals, but the seven figure income and the big-fish-in-a-big-pond lifestyle.*

Until he'd come to Wittering, met Mary and Miz Witty, Taggart had all but forgotten why he'd gone into the practice of law. To help innocent people, wrongly accused. It had been a calling, like nursing was for Mary.

"Some calling," he muttered, unable to remember when he'd done his last *pro bono* work for the public good. Certainly not since Annalisa died. "You sold out, brother—for big bucks and a luxury penthouse. Congratulations."

A knock at his door brought his head up. "Yes?"

"It's me, baby."

He experienced a stab of annoyance and peered at his watch. Eight o'clock, exactly. One thing you could say for Lee, she was punctual. He stood and crossed to the door. "Sorry. I let the time get away from me." He went into the hall and threw an arm about her shoulders, steering her toward the stairs. The last thing he wanted was to be alone in his bedroom with her.

"I was beginning to think you were avoiding me," she said.

"Of course not." It was a lie. If she hadn't deduced that by now, she wasn't the savvy legal eagle he'd given her credit for being. They descended the steps and he aimed her toward the front door. "I'll get your bags."

"Not necessary. That Jed person was here earlier. He carried them down and put them in the trunk of my car." As Taggart led her onto the porch, she slipped her arm about his waist, squeezing. "Can that guy *not* talk?"

"He's the strong, silent type," Taggart said, grateful to have the conversation turn away from them as a couple.

They crossed the porch and descended the steps to the gravel drive. "Well, I don't like that type." When they reached her car, she turned to face him, slipping her arms around his neck. "I like men who talk to me." She grinned wickedly. "The dirtier the better."

"Yeah, well..." He cleared his throat. This was the part he hated—the drawn-out, tell-me-you-love-me goodbye. Didn't she know by now she wasn't going to get what she wanted from him? His smile was courteous, but brief. "Have a good trip, Lee."

A shadow flitted over her features, but before Taggart could fully register what he saw, or be positive he saw anything, she took his face in her hands and kissed him hard on the lips. He didn't help. Reaching up, he grasped her fingers. Gently but firmly liberating his face from her grip, he clasped her hands between his and pressed her away.

"I wish you were going back with me, baby," she whispered.

"I'll be back for the Friday night meeting." He released her. "You'd better go. You know how airport security loves to frisk you."

Her gaze probed his, possibly hoping she would see something for her there. After a long moment, her expression changed subtly, her eyes glistening, her smile skewing off-center. "I wish you loved to frisk me.'' The quiet declaration held a hint of melancholy, as though somewhere, down deep, she was finally facing the truth. Taggart Lancaster was no longer her lover, and never again would be.

''Drive safely,'' he said.

Her glance shifted away for a second before she met his eyes again. ''Right.'' She lifted her hands as if to hold his face again, but seemed to think better of it, and at the last minute dropped them. Her saucy smile returned, but he knew it was a fake. The shimmer in her eyes told the true story. ''You're such a fool,'' she said, huskily.

He couldn't disagree with her, and remained silent.

She nodded slightly, a mute acknowledgment to what she now seemed to accept as true. Taggart did not love her. She swallowed and he had the feeling she was working to remove the emotion from her voice. ''Oh, baby, what you're gonna miss!'' She broke eye contact. ''Now open my car door like the Boy Scout you are.''

He did as she asked. ''Goodbye, Lee,'' he said.

''*Sayonara,* baby.'' She slid into the driver's seat, her attention focused on adjusting her skirt and fastening her seat belt. Taggart sensed she was fighting tears. Lee Stanton, the cast iron woman, was actually on the verge of crying? He experienced a gut twist of compassion, but could do nothing for her.

Even though Mary was out of his reach, for him to pretend affection for Lee, as a substitute, would do them more harm than good. Any relationship he might forge out of pity and lost hope was doomed before it began. Eventually they would hate each other. Knowing this, he made no further attempt at conversation. Closing her door, he stepped away from the car.

The rental's engine roared to life. For an instant Lee's glance met his. She winked at him, clearly attempting to appear indifferent, but the effort was faulty and hard to watch. Eyes shimmering, she quickly removed her attention to the rearview mirror, backed up and turned around. Gunning her engine, she spit chat and raised a cloud of dust.

Lee's speedy exit was a stinging memento of her frustration and anguish. The pebbles her tires spit were tantamount to assault and battery, yet Taggart felt obligated to remain there until she disappeared beyond the line of trees masking the property from the blacktop road.

When the sound of her car died away, a huge weight lifted off his shoulders. But in its place descended a shroud of nagging guilt. *Blast!* He had nothing to feel guilty about. Lee had known their affair was over before she took it upon herself to show up unannounced. Any grief she suffered she'd brought on all by herself.

For a few more seconds he stared after her, at the dust in the air. Then, without caring about where he was going, he strode into the house and up the stairs to his room. Inside, behind his closed door, he stood motionless, looking at nothing, trying not to think about anything. He had no memory of how long he remained stone-still, Mary's face floating in his mind's eye in direct disobedience to his mandate that he think about nothing. Mary was definitely *not* nothing!

She was everything.

A soft knock at his door jarred him out of his contrary fantasies. "Yes?"

"It's Mary."

He was startled—no, shocked. In all the time he'd been there, she'd never come to his door. He turned around, his mood suddenly buoyant. "Come in."

The doorknob rattled, then turned. An eternity later, she appeared, looking solemn. In her arms she held a stack of brightly wrapped gift boxes. He scanned them, neon pinks and yellows and purples, with kiddie designs, cartoon kittens, balloons and ice cream cones. Even if Mary and Taggart had been on good terms, the wrappings made it obvious the gifts weren't for him. He didn't care who they were for, the lift he got merely seeing her there, made him lighthearted, and maybe even a little light-headed. "You shouldn't have, Miss O'Mara," he kidded, stepping forward and removing her burden from her grasp. "I'm touched."

She crossed her arms, sucking in a breath. "I— I'm sorry to bother you—Bonn." She was obviously uncomfortable but trying to hide it behind a facade of civility. "Becca's coming on Friday morning, and I've been storing her birthday presents in her room. Since her birthday isn't until Sunday, I need a place to hide the gifts. Last year I hid them in the closet in here. I wondered if you'd mind—if you'd have room…"

She let the sentence die, but held eye contact. When he realized she was through speaking, he said, "Oh—sure. No problem." Turning away, he rounded his bed to the closet. Opening the door, he lifted the packages to a shelf above the clothes rod. "Any more?"

"A few."

"I'll be happy to help." He stepped out of the closet and turned toward her. She was gone. He chuckled cynically, muttering, "What did you expect, Lancaster?" Louder, he called, "Let me help."

When she didn't respond, he crossed the hall and entered the room set aside for Becca. He'd never been in there and was surprised by how perfectly it had been decorated for a little girl. The room was small, about half the size of his. Bright and airy and full of sunshine, it had a cozy, embracing feel.

The mattress of a wrought iron daybed was covered with a white, ruffled spread. A dozen or so pillows, piled against the sides and back of the bed, were clad in matching, ruffled shams. A colorful menagerie of stuffed toys lolled against the pillows.

The walls were soft pink, accented by fairy-tale artwork, hung in groupings and framed in white. The dresser, vanity table and stool were also white. A large, oval rag rug in shades of purples, pinks and greens covered most of the pine floor. The window curtains were sheer and ruffled.

Taggart nodded admiringly. "She must love this room."

His gaze met Mary's as she came out of the closet with another armload of brightly wrapped gift boxes. Her expression eased at his compliment. "She does love it." Taggart could tell Mary was picturing her half sister in her mind, because she smiled. "Becca picked out the color for the walls and we painted it together." She laughed lightly, the sound sending a quiver of desire along his spine.

Mary's gaze had gone inward, though she continued to look at Taggart. "Well, to be scrupulously honest, Becca and Pauline kept me supplied with freshly baked, chocolate-chip cookies while *I* painted.''

She continued to smile, obviously recollecting happy times with her half sister in this room. Her sweet expression, the light blush on her cheeks, affected Taggart like a particularly tough win in court—the jury's verdict so unexpected it knocked the wind from his lungs. Mary's smile affected him like that, except multiplied a thousand times. He couldn't help smiling back. Hell, he'd probably been smiling since he first saw her in his doorway.

The boxes started to slip sideways, drawing Taggart back to his offer to help. He grasped the packages, shouldering them to halt their slide. "Let me take those," he said.

She didn't let go, seeming to return from her thoughts more belatedly than Taggart. She was very close, his face inches from hers. He could tell when she returned to the here-and-now by the way her eyes went wide, and her smile vanished. "What—what are you doing?" she asked, sounding frightened.

The panic in her voice bloodied his heart. He loved this woman more than life, and she feared him, loathed him. Any declarations of who he really was, and how much he loved her, would fall on deaf ears. She wouldn't listen, and even if she heard, she wouldn't care.

Ensnared in his lie, and bitterly defeated, he had difficulty pretending that the shock on her face didn't rip him apart. He managed an apologetic grin. "Don't panic. I was just taking the packages." He lifted them away and stepped out of kissing range. "You were gone somewhere in your head and they started to fall."

She colored fiercely. "Oh—of course." Her lashes went down shyly, contritely. The effect was subtly erotic and blatantly cruel.

In an attempt at self-preservation, he glanced away. Exhibiting an ease he didn't feel, he hefted the pile of gifts. "All these are for Becca's birthday? She's a lucky little girl."

"I guess I do go a little overboard," she said. Unable to help himself, Taggart met her gaze. She still wore that charming blush. Her lips were even tilted slightly upward, an exhilarating surprise. Clearly, the closer Becca's visit came, the more elevated Mary's mood became, even in the presence of Bonner Wittering. "I started buying her gifts right after her last birthday—when I had a little extra money—after putting what I need aside for nursing courses." She shrugged, slipping her hands into her jeans pockets. "I—I guess I want to spoil her, after—after…" She shrugged again and looked away. She bit her lower lip and

Taggart could tell she was having trouble talking about Becca's circumstances.

"Yeah, I don't blame you," he said, drawing her gaze.

"You don't?" she asked, wiping away a tear.

He was surprised by her question. "Absolutely not. Why would I?"

She frowned, swallowed, then shook her head. "Joe says it's not good for her—that the real world is a hard place, and she might as well know that early."

"Please don't tell me you listen to that jerk."

"I have to," she said. "He's Becca's father."

"Well, you're her sister." Taggart wanted—no *needed*—to find words to make her smile again. "As long as she has you, she'll be okay."

Mary's gaze dropped to the rag rug and she frowned in thought. "I hope so, but Joe's hard to fight. He won't let her take half these gifts home. They'll sit here gathering dust. It's so unfair."

"If life were fair, Joe would be a grizzly bear's love-slave."

Mary's gaze shot to his face, her surprise at his comment evident in her expression. After a second, she grinned. Actually grinned. "I'd pay to see that," she said.

The shocking thrill of her smile—*aimed at him*—affected him so deeply, anything he might have planned to say lodged in his throat. A tiny glow sparked to life amid the ashes of his hope. He knew the humble flame would be fleeting and quickly flicker out, but he savored it, blessed it.

He stood there, spellbound by her smile, aware for the first time of a fragile thread that stretched between them. A connection. He sensed she felt it too—for however briefly it might endure—and a strange, spiritual peace flowed through him. He tried to memorize her face, that smile, needed to learn it by heart for the long, solitary years ahead of him.

Taggart was packed and ready to leave. He'd said goodbye to Pauline and Ruby, then had breakfast with Miz Witty and Mary, a difficult hour. Things had been different between Mary and him since the dance. Though Mary avoided him, when she could, her obvious pleasure at Becca's impending visit had an all-encompassing effect on her. Even his arrival in a room didn't dim her bubbly enthusiasm, and he'd noticed her actually smiling at him several times. He blessed Becca for that.

Mary had left to pick up her sister over thirty minutes ago. She'd be back any minute, and Taggart didn't plan to be there. It was time to go, anyway. Why drag out his agony for one more chance to see Mary's face—even if that once more would be his last chance, and would mean he could see her at her happiest.

He couldn't stay. It would be too tough on his heart, not to be able to take her in his arms, kiss those wonderful lips, make love to her, whisper how beautiful she was in the morning, or at night under the stars. Not to be able to tell her how much of the rest of his life he would give simply to glimpse again how perfect, how lovely she was, lounging sleepily in the tub, one flickering candle illuminating her body—taunting him with skin he could never touch, never kiss, never awaken to passion.

He'd heard someone say that sometimes the best thing to do was nothing at all. He hadn't understood how difficult that could be until now. He had to go back to Boston, had to leave Wittering, had to do *nothing*, never reveal his love.

He didn't know if doing nothing was kind or right or wrong or stupid or wise. He only knew he'd made, and kept, a promise to his boyhood friend, Bonner Wittering. Miz Witty believed he was her ''Bonny.'' She'd had a happy seventy-fifth birthday and a nice visit with her ''grandson.'' The game was finished and he had won.

''Yeah, right,'' he muttered, through a bitter laugh. With suffocating loss tightening his throat, he trudged down the stairs with his suitcase.

He opened the front door and was startled when Mary tumbled into his arms. Clinging, weeping, her knees buckled and she began to sink to the floor. He dropped his suitcase and lifted her in his arms. "What the—what's happened?" He carried her into the living room.

She pushed hair out of her face, and Taggart could see that she'd been crying for some time. Her eyes were red, her cheeks flushed, her face wet with tears. "She's gone—*they're gone!*" she cried, dropping her face against his shoulder, as though she were too weak and shattered to hold her head up. "The—the trailer's gone." He felt her hands fist around wads of his turtleneck shirt. "Nobody—" Her voice broke. "Nobody knew where they—they were. Just that they left sometime late Wednesday night."

"Joe's gone?" Taggart asked in disbelief. He took a seat on the velvet Victorian sofa. It creaked under their combined weight.

Seeming not to notice she sat in his lap, Mary sniffed, nodding. "And Becca—and Joe's latest girlfriend. Everything's *gone!*" She looked into Taggart's face, her expression so tragic he had a sudden, vicious urge to string Joe Lukins up by his ears.

Her fists eased and she slid her arms around his neck, crying against his chest. "By now they're out of Colorado and—and we're bordered by *seven* states! Even Texas is just a hop across the Oklahoma panhandle! They could be almost *an-*

yplace!'' she cried. "How could Joe do that? Two—two weeks is so little to ask! And Mother—wanted Becca and me to be together! The judge said..." She bit her lip and choked back a sob.

Trembling with fright and sorrow and loss, she pressed her face against his throat, her sobs muffled by his shirt. Taggart held her, stroked her hair. Scalding fury twisted his gut in a knot. How many times had he wanted to hold her, cradle her—but not like this. Not with her heart breaking.

"He—he's not supposed to leave town without letting me know where he's going," she cried. "He can't take Becca away. What—what if I never see her again?" She broke down completely, the sound of her suffering so mournful it caused him physical pain.

Taggart clenched his teeth throwing out a silent vow. *Damn you, Joe Lukins! You won't get away with this, you cowardly bastard. Maybe I can never love Mary the way I want to, but I'm a damn good lawyer with excellent contacts. I have a private investigator on retainer who can find a snowflake in Hades before it has a chance to melt. If Becca is on the face of this earth, she'll be found!*

His glance chanced across the mantel clock. Nine-thirty. *Hell,* he had to go. And not only did he have to go, but he had to go as Bonner Wittering, a man with little knowledge or interest in legal matters, except when they pertained to saving his own tail. So, as Bonner Wittering, he said, "Call the police, Mary." He knew it would do little good. The child was with her father. No all-points bulletins would be issued. No road-blocks set up. But it should be reported. Any future case she might make against Becca's father would be strengthened by verification of court-order violations.

He lay a hand on the back of her head, slowly, lovingly stroking her hair. Its light, flowery scent reminded him of the high-country meadow. He filled his lungs with the heady essence and it made him weak. Against his will, he nuzzled the side of her face with his cheek. Unable to stop himself, he placed a wayward, foolish goodbye kiss on the hair above her temple. "Joe's in the wrong," he murmured into her hair. "Report it."

He continued to stroke and caress her hair, tucking locks behind her ear that had fallen over her face. "I have to go, Mary," he whispered, his voice hoarse with regret.

He forced his hands to her shoulders, raising her into a sitting position. He felt her shudder and draw in a deep breath before she met his eyes. Sniffing, she ran her knuckles across her tear-stained cheeks. "Oh—of course," she said, her voice fragile and tremulous. "I'm sorry—I just..."

She swallowed, ran her hands through her hair to push it off her face. Breaking eye contact, she sucked in another breath to regain her poise. He had a feeling she was embarrassed for being so broken up she'd allowed herself to be comforted by "the snake." "I'll call the police right now." She scrambled off his lap and pushed up to stand. From the way she swayed and reached out for the sofa arm, it was clear she wasn't very steady.

He stood, taking her arm to help her balance. "Are you okay?"

"I'm fine." Keeping her gaze averted, she pulled out of his grasp. "Forgive me for imposing my problems on you."

He wanted to tell her that coming to him with her problems would never be an imposition, but he knew he couldn't. Instead, he said, "Don't worry about it. I've—"

"You'd better go if you're going to catch your plane," she cut in. Turning away, she hurried to the antique commode next to the living room entry and grabbed the phone.

"Right—my plane," he murmured more to himself than to Mary. She'd dismissed him from her thoughts when she turned her back. He watched her grimly. Her hands shook so badly he wasn't sure she could dial. He ached to tell her that he would do everything in his power to get Becca back, but his promise to Bonn kept him from speaking.

He stood there like a fool, lovesick and torn. His thoughts tasted like gall. He wanted to say something, do something. *Anything,* to ease her fears. "Mary, I'm sure the police will—"

"Hello? Sheriff Platt?" she said, interrupting his empty observation. "This is Mary O'Mara."

Go on! Get out! he berated inwardly. Staying any longer would be pointless. *Focus, Lancaster! You have a little girl to find—for the woman you can never have.*

CHAPTER THIRTEEN

AFTER reporting Joe Lukins' illegal, dead-of-night bolt with Becca, Mary hung up the phone. Though the sheriff was caring and sympathetic he wasn't very reassuring. It seemed, as illegal as Joe's actions might be, law enforcement put a parent absconding with his own child—no matter how big a sleazebag he might be—fairly far down on their list of priorities.

She turned around to tell Bonner the bad news only to discover he wasn't there. She jerked toward the front door. It was closed and his suitcase was nowhere to be seen. She experienced a sudden, wrenching rush of sadness.

Bonner Wittering was gone.

Well, hadn't she told him to go? Why did she think he wouldn't? And why, oh, *why* did she feel so abandoned? Why was the fact that he had actually walked away as shattering to her mind and spirit as losing Becca?

"Mary O'Mara!" she chided mournfully. "How *hopeless* can you be?" Struggling to cope with her bleak, lightless future, she sank to the

255

floor. Tears choked and blinded her. Rocking back and forth, she wept aloud.

Mary's world was shrouded in gloom. She went about her daily chores as though nothing was wrong, but inside torment ate at her. When she was with Miz Witty she did her best to be upbeat, yet every day without news of Becca pounded her spirits lower and lower.

Then, twenty-eight days from the day Joe disappeared with Becca, daylight broke through to Mary's dreary world. She got a call from authorities in Utah. A private investigator had found Becca in a small hospital there. She'd been admitted the night before with a broken arm. The PI notified the authorities of Becca's whereabouts, and they had taken charge of the matter. Exactly who the PI was, and why he'd been searching for Becca, Mary couldn't find out. She desperately wanted to thank the man, but he disappeared as quickly and furtively as he'd appeared.

What Mary did find out, to her horror, was that Joe had been in a car accident, driving drunk. He'd smashed his pickup truck into a convenience store's plate glass window. Luckily no one inside the store had been hurt.

Joe and his girlfriend suffered minor injuries, but were okay. Joe, however, was being held in the local jail. His police record from Colorado had somehow found its way to the Utah authorities. Considering Joe's long history of drinking and driving, it looked like he would be in jail for a while.

Before Mary knew what was happening, she suddenly had Becca back, at least temporarily. Then, another miracle she couldn't explain or understand came into her life in the form of the best family law attorney in Colorado. Out of the blue, he contacted her, explaining that he could get her permanent, sole custody of her half sister.

Since Mary was Becca's only other living relative, and Joe Lukins was clearly unfit as a parent and very likely headed for prison, the attorney promised ''a slam-dunk.'' His assurances lifted Mary's hopes, but she admitted she couldn't afford his services. His answer was simply, ''It's been taken care of.''

In late October, the wonderful day came when a family court judge decreed that Mary O'Mara would, now and forever, have sole custody of Becca Lukins. Mary was so overwhelmed with joy and gratitude, she impulsively hugged her lawyer. To Mary's surprise, she discovered the forceful, graying, urbane attorney, had the most charming and unexpected capacity for blushing. Unfortunately, he also had an exasperating capacity for being immovable on the subject of who hired him on Mary's behalf and who was paying for his legal expertise.

Mary suspected, of course. It had to be Miz Witty who'd orchestrated these miracles. She must have hired the PI and the attorney. There was no one else in the world who would do so much, spend so much, for Mary.

But Miz Witty kept insisting she'd done none of it. Very frustrating! Mary decided she must have the truth, once and for all. She owed Miz Witty *everything* for what she'd done. It wasn't fair that her sweet, benevolent employer wouldn't allow Mary to thank her properly. But, then, how did one thank a person for giving her everything she wanted in the whole world?

A sly, cruel voice in her head whispered, *You mean almost everything, don't you? What about Bonner Wittering?*

"Oh, stop it!" she mumbled, as she cleared lunch dishes from Miz Witty's small bedroom table. She checked her wristwatch. Becca wouldn't get out of school for another hour.

As she went back to her chore, Bonner's face loomed large in her mind's eye, making her heart leap foolishly. "Get over the man!" she groused under her breath. "Whatever chemical imbalance you're suffering, wait it out. You'll recover. And even if you don't, surely one day they'll invent a medicine to correct it—like they have for out-of-control cholesterol or rampaging blood pressure!''

''Did you say something to me, dear?'' Miz Witty asked.

Mary spun around. Had she said that out loud? ''Uh—er—no.''

Miz Witty sat before her window in her wheelchair, a novel in her hands. Snow fluttered down prettily, blanketing the pine forest behind the house. It was November third, and winter in the Rockies had begun in earnest. The older woman smiled at Mary, her expression inquisitive. ''I thought I heard...is it already time to take my blood pressure?''

Mary felt like an idiot, and shook her head. ''No—I—I was talking to myself.''

Miz Witty laughed lightly, patting the silvery mound of curls piled on her head. ''You're talking to yourself about blood pressure? Were you discussing yours or mine with yourself?''

Mary smiled wanly. ''No—my thoughts were just—um—wandering.''

Miz Witty's brow wrinkled. ''When I was your age, Mary, and my mind wandered, it certainly wasn't about blood pressure.'' She lifted a pale hand, beckoning Mary forward. ''Come here, my child.''

Mary indicated the tray of dirty dishes. ''I was going to take these to the kitchen.''

Miz Witty waved that idea away. "Forget it for the moment." She stretched out a thin, blue-veined hand. "Come, child. You look—distressed."

Mary had tried so hard to keep her irrational infatuation with Bonner from showing. But she supposed Miz Witty knew her too well to be fooled. Still, she didn't intend to discuss it. The best defense was a good offense. Stiffening her resolve, she vowed that once and for all she would get at the truth—compel Miz Witty to admit her extraordinary generosity.

She walked to her employer. "Miz Witty," she began, "I have to know the truth. You hired that lawyer, didn't you? I know I told you I didn't want any charity from you, that I wanted to make my own way. But—but finding Becca for me and then helping me get sole custody. Well, it's just so perfect. If you did this, I can't let it go as though nothing happened. I want to pay you back in some way. If you don't want money, then let me do something else. Please, I—"

"Sit down, dear," the elder woman interrupted softly, indicating the wide window seat. "I want to talk to you."

Mary was taken aback by Miz Witty's solemn request. So rarely did her employer discard her smile, Mary sensed an urgency in her, and did as she asked. "Yes?" She felt unaccountably nervous. "What is it?"

Miz Witty lowered her gaze to her book, turned it over and opened the back cover. Inside was a photograph, which she drew out and handed to Mary. It was a picture of Bonner, and another man. She looked at it, her heart soaring foolishly. Both men smiled broadly, arms slung across each other's shoulders the way brothers or good friends might do. "Why, it's Bonner." She lifted her gaze to Miz Witty. "I didn't know you had any recent snapshots of him."

Miz Witty's smile reappeared, more melancholy than happy. "Yes. It's a few years old. I'm sure Bonny doesn't even recall sending it. I found it inside a card, oh, I'd say a month before you came to work for me. It was right after my first stroke and I was in the hospital. The photograph got tucked away with the other letters and cards I received then. I ran across it last spring. I've had it in my bedside table drawer ever since." She indicated the photo. "It's a nice picture of him, isn't it?"

Mary nodded, her heart twisting. It was hard enough trying to forget Bonner when she didn't have to stare at his image—those hypnotic eyes, that devastating smile. She handed the picture back, fearing she'd burst into tears if she dared look at it any longer. "Yes—it's very nice."

Miz Witty took it, held it, gazing fondly at it. "The other man is Taggart Lancaster. He and Bonner grew up together. They're like brothers."

"They do look somewhat alike," Mary murmured.

"Yes, they do. They're handsome young men." She sighed, a sound filled with regret. "I love my grandson, Mary. His father, my only child, grew into a stern man, and he married a cold woman. They were a selfish couple, hard on Bonner because he got in the way of their pleasure. My beloved husband died when Bonn was seven. I spent years in mourning, was no help to the poor child when he needed me the most. I'm thankful he found a friend like Taggart. He's Bonner's lawyer, now, you know."

"Oh?" Mary thought she recalled hearing the name. Either Bonner or Lee must have mentioned it. "I see."

"Taggart Lancaster has been a good, stable friend." She ran a hand fondly across the photo. "Bonner needed stability in his life." She glanced up and smiled. "I know my grandson has faults, but no matter what else he might be, he has a good heart."

She gazed at the photograph again, her expression wistful. With one last caressing motion across the image, she lay the photograph inside the back cover and shut her book.

When she faced Mary again, she smiled tenderly. "I love you like my own granddaughter, and though I would be happy to pay for your nursing courses, or anything else you might need, I have respected your wishes that you pay your own way." She reached out, covering Mary's hand with hers. "You must believe me when I say I did not hire the private investigator nor did I hire the attorney." She squeezed Mary's fingers affectionately. "My grandson may have many faults, Mary, but if I know him at all, I also know he has powerful friends."

Mary was confused. "Are you saying you think Bonner did it?"

Miz Witty withdrew her hand from Mary's. "I can't be sure of anything." She paused, then added, "What other explanation could there be?"

Mary had no idea. "I can't believe it." She frowned at Miz Witty, dubious. "Besides, aren't you sending him money? If he hired them, then ultimately you would be paying for it. You'd know."

Miz Witty lifted her hands, as though mystified. "All I can say is, Bonner has not asked me for a penny since Joe took Becca away."

Mary chewed the inside of her cheek, her frustration at explosive levels. "Well, one way or the other, I need to know."

"Why don't you ask him?"

Mary's gaze had dropped to her lap, where she clutched her hands together. With Miz Witty's question, her attention shot up and their eyes met. "You mean—*call Bonner?*"

Miz Witty smiled, her expression compassionate. "A moment ago you were willing to do anything for me, if I'd hired the private investigator and lawyer. Now you're horrified at the idea of picking up a phone?"

Mary felt a blush creep up her cheeks. How small could she be? "Of—of course, you're right. I'm being silly." She cleared her throat, telling herself she was a grown-up, a mature person. She could do this. She could speak to Bonn on the phone without falling apart. "I'll call—right now."

She got up and went to Miz Witty's bedside table. Bonner's number was programmed into speed dial. She pressed the button, telling her heart to slow down or she would be unconscious before the call could go through.

She concentrated on breathing slowly, deeply as the phone began to ring. Almost instantly it went to an answering machine; a metallic male voice requested that she leave a message. She licked her lips, nervous. What could she say? What possible message could she leave? Before she gave herself time to think about it, she slammed down the receiver.

"Did you change your mind?"

Mary shook her head, furious with herself for her cowardice. "He's not there." So much for being a mature adult. She'd been too frightened and tongue-tied to leave a simple message, like— *Call me. We have to talk!* Blood pounded in her ears and her face burned with humiliation. She couldn't bear to face Miz Witty. Hurrying to the table, she grabbed the tray of dishes. "I—I'll try again—later." She dashed out the door.

Mary did try, and try. She really did! For three days she called, over and over, and was answered by the awful machine, its metallic monotone demanding the same thing—leave a message! Her response was invariably the same—a dry, croaking nothing. Even when she wrote down exactly what she planned to say and was determined to speak, she could only manage a brief, high-pitched croak, then silence.

In desperation, she'd finally called Bonner's lawyer's office. His secretary told her Mr. Lancaster was in court. When Mary asked if she knew whether Bonner was out of town, the secretary hesitated, then said, she wasn't at liberty to give out information about clients. Because of the secretary's delay before responding to something that should have been automatic, Mary got an odd, nagging feeling, as though the woman knew where Bonner Wittering was, and the news wasn't good.

Was Bonner in trouble?

Mary felt a headache coming on, a dull throbbing she couldn't get rid of. She was tired, angry with herself and depressed to discover what a spineless baby she was. If Bonner had really done so much for her, the least she could do was summon the courage to thank him! And what was a phone call, after all? How did a person thank someone over the phone for such a grand and caring gift?

Maybe the reason she hadn't been able to speak to that dratted machine was because she knew it was the cowardly way out. So what if she went weak at the sound of his name? So what if she felt a mad, unruly attraction for him? If he'd been the one to facilitate Becca's return, and hired the lawyer who'd won her sole custody of her half sister, didn't he deserve her face-to-face thanks?

No matter how hard it might be to see him again, he deserved to be told in person. And if he was in trouble—and the sick feeling in her stomach told her he was—maybe she could help, at least offer moral support. He might be a conniver and a playboy, but if he were truly responsible for giving her back her half sister, she owed him that, and a lot more. With her resolve set, she knocked on Miz Witty's door.

"Come in?"

Once inside, Mary stood tall and faced her employer, who sat at her antique writing desk. "Miz Witty, I've decided to go to Boston, to speak to Bonner in person."

Miz Witty's face brightened. "Why, that's a fine idea, child."

"After thinking over what you said, I know in my heart finding Becca must be Bonner's doing. A few words over the phone aren't enough. What he did was too important, too wonderful for—"

"I hope you won't mind, Mary," Miz Witty broke in. Reaching in her top desk drawer, she pulled out an envelope. "I took the liberty of purchasing an airline ticket to Boston." She held it out. "For you."

CHAPTER FOURTEEN

ON A chilly Friday afternoon, Mary took a taxi from the Boston airport to the apartment building where Bonner lived. Inside, the security guard at a desk was more forthcoming than Taggart Lancaster's secretary. The young man seemed almost gleeful to pass along the word that Bonner Wittering had been convicted of insider trading, had his bond revoked since his conviction because of the increased flight risk, and had been in jail. He went on to say Bonner was in court *this very minute* for the punishment hearing.

Mary was horrified by the news. What in heaven's name was insider trading, and what kind of punishment did it involve? After coaxing the security guard to stash her suitcase, Mary took her taxi to the federal courthouse. She had no idea what she thought she might do once she got there. She needed to see Bonner, hopefully get a chance to speak with him.

But convicted! That had to mean prison! She'd known he was a lot of things, but a criminal? The man who'd treated Miz Witty with such respect and thoughtfulness, the man who'd been kind, even while rejecting Pauline, the man who'd gone to great and costly lengths to get Becca back? Could this man be a criminal? It didn't seem possible.

As Mary's cab approached the courthouse, she stared in awe. Most of Wittering's main street could have been set down inside the magnificent brick and granite edifice. Located on Fan Pier, the imposing building overlooked Boston Harbor.

As Mary scanned the courthouse, she was reminded of the sea and sailing ships, from the towering rotunda, which looked like a lighthouse, to the multistory, concave window-wall, created by hundreds of panes of glass. Reminiscent of a huge sail, it allowed a spectacular view of the harbor.

Upon entering the cavernous rotunda, she asked an official where the Bonner Wittering punishment hearing was going on, and was given directions. Frightened, and unsure why, she hurried up the curved, sweeping granite stairway in the main lobby. The place became a blur and she blinked back tears. Why, oh why, did she have to be in love with a man who, at this very moment, was doubtlessly being sentenced to prison? She stumbled, almost falling, but righted herself.

And why did she have to choose *this minute* to face the truth—that she loved Bonner Wittering? It wasn't a happy discovery! Now that she'd faced it, what was she going to do?

She burst into a run; her high-heels echoed over the granite floor in a massive hallway that looked like a downtown sidewalk. Around her people paced, or hunched on benches lining the walkway. The men and women she passed looked as serious and tense as she felt, few taking notice of the spectacular panorama of Boston Harbor and the distant, downtown skyline, beyond the window-wall.

When she reached the courtroom where Bonner's hearing was being held, she swallowed hard, gathered her courage and pushed through the door. Her heart hammering in her throat, she made herself as inconspicuous as possible at the rear of the wood-paneled room. She scanned the place; it looked like a trial was going on, but there were no people in the jury box, and nobody sat in the witness stand. A man stood before the judge, speaking passionately, his voice ringing in the chamber, deep and rich and powerful.

Mary focused on him, tall, straight, in an expensive looking navy suit. Though his back was to her, she felt a tingle of awareness. It raced up and down her spine, startling her. The man's words hadn't registered, except for their sound. But now inflection and intonation penetrated her consciousness, and Mary stared, stunned.

That was Bonner's voice.

"Your Honor, my client, Bonner Wittering, has had a great deal of time to come to understand the gravity of his actions, however inadvertently and unwittingly he became involved...."

Mary watched as the speaker turned toward a seated man, indicating him with a broad gesture. He continued to speak, his voice full of conviction, but Mary couldn't comprehend the words. Her mind whirled with bewilderment. The man she knew to *be* Bonner Wittering was speaking *about* Bonner Wittering, and seemed to be identifying another person *as* Bonner Wittering.

A young, casually dressed male stood nearby, engrossed in what was being said. She sidled over to him, and whispered, "Who is that—that person speaking?"

The observer briefly glanced her way, then returned his attention to the speaker. "That's Taggart Lancaster."

Mary stared in shock at the stranger at her side. It was one thing to think the world had gone topsy-turvy, but to discover it actually *had* was extremely alarming. Mary refused to allow the statement to compute in her mind. When she finally managed to speak, her voice was raspy. "You—you mean Bonner Wittering, don't you?"

The man peered at her again, his expression cautioning. "Wittering's the defendant, lady," he whispered. "Now kindly keep quiet. I'm studying to be a criminal defense lawyer, and Lancaster's the best.''

Lancaster's the best.

That statement rattled around in Mary's head for several minutes as she stared at the man speaking so eloquently to the judge, a white-haired female who also appeared to be listening intently. Mary looked around, noticing the entire courtroom was completely still, enthralled—the spectators, bailiff, prosecuting attorney, and the defendant, Bonner Wittering. Only the court reporter moved, his fingers flying. Everyone else appeared engrossed in Taggart Lancaster's words.

As he spoke, he took a few steps toward the judge's bench. After a moment, he turned around, faced the spectators as he once again indicated his client. Moving back to the defense table, his gaze lifted to skim the crowd. The instant his eyes met hers, Mary felt it—by the blow to her heart.

She knew the second he registered who she was, because he paused, midsentence. For one, tiny grain of time, Taggart Lancaster came to a complete, astonished halt. She felt it more than saw it, because almost at once, he finished his sentence and his stroll to the defense table, lifted a sheaf of papers, faced the judge and went on with his exhortation.

Mary felt disoriented, ripped up by conflicting emotions. Bonner hadn't visited Wittering at all!

His lawyer had! *Taggart Lancaster had!* Voices screamed in her head, muted and sharp at the same time.

Taggart Lancaster wasn't a playboy or a spendthrift or rash. But he was a lowlife who kept wealthy, spoiled clients out of trouble with his silver-tongued spin on their crimes. And, even worse as far as Mary was concerned, he'd perpetrated a huge fraud on Miz Witty!

Or had he? She recalled the photograph her employer had shown her—*of both men.*

Then Miz Witty must have known all along…

Mary squeezed her eyes shut and shook her head, not knowing what to think or how to feel. Did the fact that Miz Witty knew Taggart wasn't Bonner excuse what they did? She was so disconcerted and bewildered and upset, she didn't know who to be angry at, or how angry to be. She felt stifled. The room seemed suddenly overheated. She had trouble breathing, was seeing double.

In an anguished daze, she stumbled out of the courtroom and darted down the hall, running blind. Before she knew it, she was outside. The wind had picked up and it had grown bitingly cold with the approaching dusk.

She pulled her woolen suit jacket close about her and walked aimlessly. She didn't know how long she wandered before she found herself standing in front of a coffee shop. Shivering from her emotional wretchedness and the evening chill, she went inside. She had to think, get her thoughts straight. She'd come to Boston to thank Bonner for what he'd done for her and Becca. But now what? Who did she thank—and who did she strangle?

Taggart had a hard time focusing on Bonner's defense. The instant he saw Mary, his brain turned to ashes. She was here, in Boston, in the same room with him, but he couldn't take her in his arms. He couldn't hold her the way he had— in his dreams—for the past three, eternal months. He lived for the night and the escape it brought, because those were the only hours when he felt hope or joy.

Get your mind on straight, he warned inwardly. *Finish this! You care about Bonner. Even though this is your swan song as his attorney-slash-baby-sitter, you still owe him your best. Don't let him down!*

Taggart had done a lot of soul-searching since he left Wittering, Colorado. He'd decided to downsize his practice, move west. Open a little law office in the Rockies. Let the simple, country life wipe the city grime from his soul. He wanted to help plain folk with their troubles, get into *pro*

bono child advocacy work. He needed to feel ful-
filled, clean.

Today's punishment hearing was the end of his
prestigious and lucrative Boston practice, as well
as the end of his lawyer/client relationship with
Bonner, if not quite the end of their friendship.
He still loved Bonn like a brother. But he knew
he couldn't spend the rest of his life holding
Bonner's hand. It wasn't good for either of them.
Taggart needed a life of his own and Bonner had
to face life on his own and learn to accept responsibility for his actions.

The next hour dragged by like an ice age.
When Taggart looked for Mary again, she was no
longer in the courtroom. Where had she gone? He
needed to find her, if only to be near her once
more. To catch the high-meadow sweetness of her
scent, to look into those smoky eyes that haunted
him, day and night. He knew she must be furious—discovering the lie. But he was accustomed
to her dislike for him. It didn't diminish the way
he felt about her, fool that he was.

At last, the hearing was over and the judge's
decision rendered. Taggart instructed his assistant
to pack up, and left the courtroom as quickly as
he could, determined to find Mary. He prayed she
hadn't rushed back to the airport and caught the
first plane leaving Massachusetts.

Just outside the courtroom door, he practically ran into her. Her cheeks were flushed, her hair wind-tossed. She'd obviously gone somewhere, then decided to return. He was grateful for that, even if she'd only come back to slap his face.

"Mary," he said, unable to keep from smiling. "I was looking for—"

"Just exactly who are you!" she demanded, chin high.

For a second he'd forgotten everything but his relief that she hadn't bolted for parts unknown. "Oh—right." His smile died, and he nodded in understanding. "About that…"

"Never mind about that! I don't know why I even askcd, because I never want to speak to you again!" Her angry expression altered slightly and she winced, as though having a thought she wasn't completely happy about. "But—but before I go, I need to know who hired the PI and the lawyer to get Becca back? Was it Bonner?"

Remorse twisted his gut. Mary still found him detestable. That reality plunged him into gloom. Why admit he hired the PI and called in some favors to hire the best family law expert in Colorado to get Mary's half sister for her? The last thing he wanted from her was grudging indebtedness. "I'm Bonner's lawyer," he said solemnly, "not his father. I don't know everything he does."

Mary stared, her frown dubious. "Don't give me that malarkey. My guess is you know more about what Bonner does than Bonner knows!"

Taggart heard a sound at his back and realized the courtroom door had burst open. A second later an arm fell heavily across his shoulders. "I can't believe you kept me out of the clink that time, man! That stuff you said about me was brilliant. You almost had the prosecutor in tears. I'm practically a saint."

"I wouldn't go quite that far." Taggart peered at his friend. "And you're not scot-free, old buddy. You have five years of probation to serve. And Judge Bancroft's ruling was damned imaginative."

"Well, it's not jail." Bonner's glance gravitated to Mary. Taggart watched his features change from kidding to lecherous. "My, my, who's this?"

Taggart looked at Mary who was watching Bonner, her expression curious. He had a feeling she guessed she was finally looking at Miz Witty's real grandson. "Mary O'Mara, this is the infamous Bonner Wittering."

Bonn laughed, slapped Taggart's shoulder, his gaze remaining on Mary. "He means *interesting*. Poor slob's never been good with words." He held out a hand. "It's a true pleasure to meet you, Mary."

Taggart wasn't surprised that Bonner didn't recognize the name. Typical of his live-for-the-moment mentality, once the problem was solved, he forgot Mary was the one who'd written the intimidating ''out of the will'' letters.

Taggart could tell when Mary came to the same realization. Her gaze flashed to meet his, fiery indignation and glittery gratitude illuminated her eyes in an amazing display. In that one instant, she knew Bonner had no idea who she was, and therefore, couldn't have been responsible for helping her and Becca. Her attention returning to Bonn, she politely accepted his hand. ''Mr. Wittering,'' she said. ''The pleasure is all *yours*.''

Removing her hand from his grasp, she shifted her gaze to Taggart. ''Then I really do have you to thank for Becca?'' She looked pained, almost pleading that it not be true. He was sickened to see how desperately she didn't want to be indebted to a sleazy, rat-rescuing lawyer.

''What's going on?'' Bonner cut in, removing his arm from about Taggart's shoulders and facing him. ''What did you do to this lovely woman to make her angry with us?''

Taggart grunted out a caustic chuckle and shook his head at his friend. ''She's the *Mary* who works for your grandmother. The one who wrote you the letters. Remember?''

Bonner looked surprised and glanced at her in disbelief. "Her?" he asked. "She's the crotchety old battle-ax you went out there to sweet talk?"

"That's why you wanted me to go, not why I went," Taggart said. "And I'm afraid even your charm won't be enough this time. She hates us, and with good reason." He held a hand toward his friend. "Good luck Bonn. Make this work. You can turn your life around."

Bonner accepted Taggart's hand, though he frowned. "You're not serious about being through as my lawyer. What'll I do without you, man?"

They shook hands and Taggart released his grip. "You'll grow up."

Bonner peered at Mary, transferring his scowl to her. "Ah, I think the dawn just broke." He cocked his head, eyeing her critically. "Honey, if I can be credited with any brains at all, then I'm guessing you're the reason Tag's causing me all this grief."

She met his accusing frown, her defiance changing to confusion. "What?"

Bonner indicated Taggart with a brusque wave. "Hell, Tag's leaving Boston and a big money law firm, moving west to have some hand-to-mouth, hick practice in the mountains. Craziest of all, he says he wants to do free legal stuff for kids, or some such nonsense, while he leaves *me* here to fend for myself!'' He thumped Taggart on the arm. ''Dang! Five years' probation doing community service as athletic coach of an inner city recreational club.'' He shook his head. ''All those grubby kids. I don't know, man. Now that I think on it, maybe I'd be better off in jail.''

Taggart experienced a rush of compassion for his friend and managed a brief grin. ''No, you wouldn't. You'll be a great athletic director. You love sports and the kids will love you. You're a funny guy—a good *man,* Bonn. I have faith in you.''

He turned to Mary. Her stiffened stance and critical expression told him all too clearly there was little left to say between them. He was suddenly bone-weary. Seeing her again, knowing his love for her was without hope, reopened the wound inside him, and oh, how it bled. He ached to hold her, but resisted, stuffing his hands into his slacks pockets.

With a brisk nod of farewell, he murmured, ''Goodbye Miss O'Mara.''

CHAPTER FIFTEEN

MARY reeled from everything Bonner had said. She was having trouble absorbing it all.

Taggart's swift exit gave him a hefty head start. When she realized he was gone, she dashed after him. Why couldn't she let him go? Why did she feel an urgent need to catch him? Why was she tugging on his suit sleeve? "What did he mean when he said you're leaving your law firm and moving west? You're not going to set up a law practice in Colorado—are you?"

"Yes, I am." He continued to walk rapidly, and Mary had to run to keep up.

Her heart fluttered at the thought of Bonn—er—Taggart Lancaster being so close, but she couldn't ignore the fact that he'd pretended to be Bonner, to play Miz Witty for a fool, even if she had known all along he wasn't her grandson.

"How could you go along with Bonner's scheme to cozy up to Miz Witty for his inheritance?" she demanded.

"How could I..." Taggart came to a halt, turning on her. "Why do you think I told Bonner I couldn't be his lawyer anymore?" His tone was harsh. "I thought he only wanted to ease her last days. When I found out he'd conned me, sent me there to insure his place in her will, I told him that was the last straw. I was quitting. I'd get him through this insider trading mess, but that was it."

Mary could see the truth glowing in his eyes. Those earthy eyes had always confused her with what looked like, but couldn't be, genuine sincerity. She realized now that the whole time, in all things but the name he'd gone by, he *had* been sincere, in everything he'd said or done.

"I called Miz Witty and told her the truth," he went on. "She said she knew I wasn't Bonner, but decided to play along."

"Why?" Mary asked, dumbfounded.

He hailed a cab and Mary instinctively jumped in with him.

"Where are you going?" He looked as puzzled to see her there as she felt.

"I don't know—yet," she said, very confused, yet strangely giddy. "Did Miz Witty say why she played along?"

He frowned, glanced away for an instant, then turned back to watch her intently. "Something about thinking you and I would make a nice couple."

Mortified, Mary couldn't look him in the eyes. Had Miz Witty sensed how Mary felt? From the first moment she'd met Taggart Lancaster, she'd tried to hate him, but failed miserably. She blinked, gathering her courage and poise.

He was close. She could feel his heat and it made her feel good. She was glad simply to be near him, no matter how foolish that gladness might be. "What about Lee?" she asked, reluctantly returning her gaze to his.

"What about her?" he asked.

"Is she willing to move to Colorado?"

"I hope not." He looked as though he'd never told a truer truth in his life.

Mary watched him with bewilderment. "But, she as much as told me you were getting married."

"Not to her."

"Not to her?" she echoed.

"No," he whispered, his gaze holding hers in its soft grasp. "Lee said a lot of things—stupid things."

Recalling Lee's cruel assertion that he'd laughed at her the whole time he'd been in Wittering, she had to ask, "Was one of the stupid things, that you thought I had a naive crush on you, and you found it funny?"

He looked shocked. "What?"

She experienced an odd upwelling of emotion. Was it a frantic surge of longing? Of hope? "Then you weren't laughing at me?"

He shook his head. "No. Never," he murmured, in the gathering darkness. "I told Lee you hated me, whether you knew me as Bonner Wittering, playboy, or Taggart Lancaster, high-priced shyster." He paused for a heartbeat, then went on, "It was never funny, Mary. Believe me, every day I hated myself—and the lie—more and more." His assertion held great depth of emotion and honest regret. Suddenly, Mary no longer doubted him, could no longer find anything to dislike about him, and a great sorrow lifted away.

"Lee was angry, spiteful." His compelling eyes held her prisoner. She could hardly breathe. "You see, I told her I didn't love her. I also told her who I do love."

She leaned toward him, compelled by some foolish longing. "You did?" Her throat was dry, her words scratchy.

"Yes," he whispered. "I told her—I love you."

Her heart thumped erratically. The noise was so loud she knew she must have heard wrong. "Who?" she asked, barely able to make a sound.

His expression serious, his dark eyes probing, he said, "You, Mary. I love you. From the first moment I saw you, I was lost." His nearness, the shimmer in his eyes, was the answer to a prayer.

He took her hand, lifted it, brushing his lips across her knuckles. She began to tingle with anticipation, with need. "I didn't think it could happen again," he murmured.

His last word caught her off guard. "Again?"

He nodded. "I was married—for three years. Three perfect years. After Annalisa died—I didn't even hope..." The sentence tapered off, and Mary sensed he was having difficulty retaining his composure. "Then suddenly there you were, and my heart was yours."

His gaze was as gentle as a caress, his eyes sad. "I know you hate me, but I hoped, maybe one day you might forgive me. And if I were in Wittering, practicing law—helping children, and people like your dad, get justice—that we might..." His words vaguely unsteady, he let the sentence die away.

She stared. His disclosure was slow to register on her dizzied senses. "You—you love me?" she asked in disbelief. Did he really say it, or had she finally gone around the bend to complete insanity?

He nodded. "More than life."

He held her hand. The act was so sweet, so pure, she wanted to cry. Strange new, miraculous thoughts began to race through her mind. "You love *me*?" she repeated, her voice cracking with emotion. She adored the sound of it but had a hard time believing.

He smiled, the expression melancholy, charmingly so. "Don't be so shocked. It isn't—*necessarily* catching."

Her heart soared into heaven. The beauty of his quiet admission filled her heart, restored her soul. "But—but it is!" she cried, then shook herself. How could she blurt such an idiotic remark? "I mean—I love you. I didn't want to, but—but I couldn't help myself."

He stared for a moment, wordlessly, his look so galvanizing it sent a current of electricity zinging through her. Then, like sunshine breaking through after a bitter ice storm, his smile appeared. Somewhere on high, Mary was sure she could hear a chorus of angels burst into song.

"Well, then..." He took her face between his big, warm hands. "I have a question I want to ask you."

She cupped her hands over his, her whole being filled with a radiant, new peace. "Ask away."

"I was hoping—a little nursing student with a wicked temper might consent to marry me." He paused, his expression going serious. "If she'll have a reformed shyster who is tired of saving rats from sinking ships."

She studied his lean, sharp-edged face. Happy tears came to her eyes. "I think I can speak for her..." Slipping her arms about his neck, she brought him closer. "...when I say—yes—*oh, yes* my darling. I wouldn't have it any other way."

He took her in his arms. "I love you, Mary O'Mara. I'll love you forever and ever..."

His vow of undying passion tasted hot and sweet against her lips—a delicious prelude to paradise.

MILLS & BOON® PUBLISH EIGHT LARGE PRINT TITLES A MONTH. THESE ARE THE EIGHT TITLES FOR OCTOBER 2003

———————— ❦ ————————

A RICH MAN'S REVENGE
Miranda Lee

THE TOKEN WIFE
Sara Craven

THE GREEK'S SECRET PASSION
Sharon Kendrick

HIS AFTER-HOURS MISTRESS
Amanda Browning

THE ITALIAN MILLIONAIRE'S MARRIAGE
Lucy Gordon

SURRENDER TO A PLAYBOY
Renee Roszel

HIS CONVENIENT FIANCÉE
Barbara McMahon

THE BRIDAL BET
Trish Wylie

MILLS & BOON®

Live the emotion

0903 Rom